HIS TO MATE

NEW EARTH
BOOK TWO

SELINA COFFEY
SUMMER COOPER

LOVY BOOKS

Lovy Books Ltd
20-22 Wedlock Road
London N1 7GU
United Kingdom.

Cover by SC Creative

*W*hat was the date?

Some month, some day, 2025. Was it the end of April? Or maybe it was May? It could even possibly be July.

Ann searched around in her brain, calculated weeks and months, but still couldn't think of what the exact date might be. It didn't really matter, she supposed, but it would be nice to have an idea. Then she could calculate… things.

She rested her elbows on the fine mahogany secretary in the study and put her head in her hands. She could always make a new calendar up or go by the one that Rager and his people brought with them.

"What are you up to in here, Ann?" Rager's voice cut into her thoughts and she turned with a smile.

"I'm trying to figure out what today is. I've lost track

of the date, somehow." She held her face up for his kiss and paused when he stroked her cheek with his thumb. He had on his uniform still, but the gloves were gone, and she felt the smooth touch of his skin against hers with delight.

Those orange eyes of his glowed for a second before the flare died down and he smiled. "Why do you need to know what the date is?"

"I don't, really. I just like to keep track of things and knowing the date helps with that."

"What kind of things?" The cat-like eyes that so distracted her narrowed now and traced down to her lips.

"Like when the plants will produce food, when it might start cooling off. Will it cool off?" She stopped checking things off on her fingers and tilted her head. "Has what you've done changed the climate in a permanent way? Will it always be this warm or will we have seasons?"

"There will be seasons, just like there will be tides. Things won't be exactly the same as they were before your cataclysm, but they will be... similar." He finally moved away and went to sit on the black leather sofa in front of the fireplace. They kept the fires going out of habit from the cold days, and because it helped drive up electricity consumption.

The newly restored power plants produced far too

much electricity. So, they'd all been advised to burn fires in at least one room and to keep the air conditioners on. Ann liked the fires, because it was a tie to their old life, to the days when survival was all that mattered. She went to the fire now, to stir the glowing embers that had once been trees into a pile before she put new wood on to catch alight instantly.

"Good, I like having seasons." She felt the familiar tug to go back to where he stood, to wheedle her way into his embrace if she had to. She'd learned to control it, a little, but she knew it wouldn't be long before she was little more than a puddle at his feet. That's what happened every single day since they'd married.

She craved him like she craved air, and it was far more than just a momentary need that could be soothed with a soft touch or a kiss. She had this drive, this instinct to take everything from him that she could, while she gave everything she had in return. He felt it too, although he was a lot better at hiding it than she was.

"What are we having for dinner tonight?" he asked as he came up behind her.

She stood up, smoothed down the lines of the dark blue linen dress she wore, a creation that swirled flirtatiously around her ankles, and tilted her head back to look up at him. "A vegetarian dish I found in an old recipe book. It looks really good, and we had all of the ingredients, so I asked that to be made for us."

"Hm, alright. That would use fewer resources than constantly relying on meat, I suppose." He went to the area behind the sofa and poured himself a glass of scotch. "Want one?"

"No, thank you. I haven't eaten in a while; it will go straight to my head."

"Maybe I want it to, my sweet." He looked over at her with that smirky glint in his eye, and she knew his control had slipped.

"Not before dinner." She gave him a mock glare and went back to the secretary to sit down. It was all part of the game, however. To test him, to see how long he could resist before he took her, the way he wanted to. The way *she* wanted him to.

"Fine, not before dinner." He stretched out the long length of his legs before he crossed them at the ankles. "But as soon as dinner has finished…"

Ann glanced at him from beneath her lashes, a smug smile on her lips. "As soon as dinner has finished."

"Good. Now, how is your family?" He let his head fall back on the couch as if he didn't really care, but she could see by the way his head tilted towards her that he did. He was just a very tired man.

"They're fine." She had gone back to see her mother earlier in the day, but she hadn't seen Rex or Amanda, only her mother. "She's had the tomato plants put in and she's got plans for more. We'll have vegetables coming out of our ears before long."

Ann picked her pen back up and began to draw lines on a blank sheet of paper. Seven columns, four rows, that's all she needed for now. How to start though? She thought about it for a moment, tapped the edge of the pen against her jaw, and then wrote in the day her last period happened, two weeks ago. Which meant she was due for another one in two more weeks.

I'm not stupid, she thought, as she looked down at her calendar. She knew what the rhythm method was, and how to calculate when she could become pregnant. The problem was, she had no way to prevent it at the moment, other than that method. When you couldn't say no, because your body wouldn't let you, well, the chances were high that she'd become pregnant quickly.

Was she pregnant even now? Surely, not. She'd like to get to know the man a little before they made it to that stage. With a sigh, she looked down at the paper. She knew her duty to this alien overlord was to breed, that was her sole purpose, really. Trying to deny that would just be stupid. Something she wasn't.

If it happened, it happened, she decided, and put the paper in the fire. If only she felt as cavalier as that though. Her face twisted and for a moment, she thought she might cry. Maybe she didn't need to know the date so much, after all.

"What's wrong, Ann?" Rager asked from behind her, and she took a deep breath to calm her nerves. With a twist of her neck and a roll of her eyes, the tears that had threatened were gone and she turned to him with a smile on her face.

"Just a headache that some food will cure. Shall we head to the dining room?" She had to pretend she was eager for food, but her hunger for him was something she didn't have to fake at all. As soon as their eyes met, it was there between them, hot and alive. But on hold. Until they'd had their dinner. A smile tugged at the corners of her mouth, and she linked her arms with his when he stood.

"If the food doesn't cure it, I know something that might." His words were a silky whisper above her ear, and she leaned into his shoulder.

"Hm, I bet you do." She turned to face him, a flirtatious smile in place. "But food first."

They walked together, hand in hand, to the dining room. Five years ago, any other 20-year-old American woman would be freaking out about being forced to marry an alien. Especially one that had come to her in her dreams before she'd even met him. But that was five years, and an entirely different world, ago. She'd survived the Earth's greatest cataclysm since humanity first learned to stand upright. She'd lived in a bunker and watched as a new ice age came, then went, in the blink of an eye.

Since they'd left their home all those years ago, Ann had learned to adjust, to think on her feet, and most importantly, to adapt. Sometimes that was the best direction to go in, to wait and see, to go with the flow instead of fighting against the tide. It didn't hurt that Rager was drop-dead gorgeous with a talent for all things… pleasurable.

Ann's smile went from a mask to hide her real thoughts to one of honest desire. She glanced at him as they sat down at the table and a wolf servant came in to fill their glasses with cold water. A bottle of wine sat at Rager's elbow, already opened and ready to pour. She glanced around the now familiar room.

It was softly lit, full of dark woods and antique luxury, a dining room that could host a statesman or a celebrity. The table filled the room, a massive thing that she could climb on and crawl across for a few feet before she got to the end. Or to her mate.

Her eyes flicked to Rager and she felt the heat that now made her cheeks glow. He'd created a monster within her, one that was hungry, even when it was asleep. For a few minutes he could fill that monster, put it to rest, but it didn't take long before the monster was hungry again.

She'd had no idea that thoughts of sex could fill your head so very much. Before she'd started to dream about him, she'd sometimes had sex dreams, and she'd had the occasional fantasy about Rex, but she hadn't been so… hungry. Her need for him was more than want, it was a real need, something that sometimes distracted her, even when she was busy.

"You know if you keep looking at me like that, I won't be able to eat, don't you? And I'm very hungry, my dear." His deep voice was soft, yet she could still hear the gravelly huskiness of it.

Her heart skipped a beat and she looked at him, brown eyes met orange, and before she knew it, she was on her feet and doing just what she'd thought about a moment ago. She crawled along the table until her face was right in front of his. The monster inside had broken free and rather than subservient, she felt incredibly powerful.

With a careful hand, she pushed the wine behind her, along with his tableware and the glass. Carefully, she moved until her feet were on the arms of his chair. With a teasingly lifted brow, she brought her gaze to his, despite the blush on her cheeks, and leaned back on her right hand. "Then we can't let you go hungry now, can we?"

"Oh. Indeed, we can't." His tongue flicked across his

lips and his eyes went down. "I won't go hungry at all with that pretty pussy to eat, will I?"

"I don't think you will."

He tapped a device on his arm and gave an order. "Hold dinner until I say otherwise."

To her surprise, Rager pushed his chair back to make room and dropped to his knees in front of her. With a guttural grunt, he pulled her legs up close to his head, until she was situated just right for his attention. She felt his hot breath first, along her right thigh, before it wafted over her damp skin. She was always ready for him; this moment was no different.

"Show me what you want, Ann. Guide me. Take what you want." His orange eyes were two flames in his face, and they drew her in.

"I want..." her bravado faltered, and she swallowed hard. He'd said to show him. Her left hand came up and reached for his hair.

He'd never been cruel to her. He'd never hurt her. The idea that this was a test, that he'd take her hand in his in anger was silly. He'd never given her reason to even think that thought. Another hard swallow and she let her fingers tighten in his dark hair before she guided his head... down.

"Here, I want you here." Her voice was ragged, laced with desire and fear as her heart raced in her chest.

"Then that's what you shall have, Ann." His lips

played over her delicate skin as he spoke, and her hips jerked to meet the promised touch. "Mm, you smell delicious, Ann."

His tongue flicked out and lapped at her skin, a slide of wet heat that made her breath catch in her chest. She couldn't stop the low moan that started deep in her chest, a sound of deep pleasure. When his tongue curled around that blissful spot that made her toes curl against the chair, she fell back against the table and jutted her hips so that his tongue would press harder against it.

"Right there, don't move, just," Ann paused as he did something that made her nails clench against the cold, hard surface of the oak table. "Don't stop."

She heard the sound of his satisfaction at her response and felt the hum of it as a new thrill against her sensitive skin. He had only touched her there, but already the world had zoomed into nothing more than him, her, and his tongue on her clit.

There were no more words as he worked her expertly, with no fumbled caresses, only the sure touch of a man that knew exactly what he was doing. Her hips started to dance in time with his tongue, and that ache started to work into her blood, into every organ in her body as she waited, just there. She only needed a moment longer, she thought, and realized she was holding her breath.

Just one more second, was her last thought as she

took a deep breath and the world became nothing more than liquid pleasure that rolled throughout her body straight into her brain. She gasped his name as her back arched off the table. She couldn't help it, her body moved by instinct alone as it reached to prolong that second of euphoria. She gasped when another wave shook her, and her body twisted when it came yet again. She'd wanted to show him who was in control, she wanted to break his control, but as she rode yet another wave to that dark place that only real pleasure can take you to, she knew she had lost.

Rager was the one in control, and nothing could change that. Good thing she didn't mind being the loser, she thought with a satisfied grin.

2

Ann woke up the next morning with a smile on her face. Rager's attentions had kept her up until the late hours, but she didn't care. It wasn't like she had anywhere to be today. The servants had their assigned duties, she had no appointments, and the day was hers. After a long, hard night, some time in a hot bubble bath with a book was all she really wanted.

She stretched as she thought about what she'd order for breakfast and looked over to Rager's pillows when her hand brushed against something. It was a white box with a red bow and a smile twitched her lips. A present?

She sat up and pulled the ribbon apart to open the box. Her mouth dropped open when she saw what it was. A piece of paper fell out to reveal an MP3 player, new earbuds, and a charger! A soft shriek of happiness filled the air as she put the earbuds in and hit play. It didn't matter which song played first, all that mattered was hearing something that she knew. She pressed a button on her nightstand to let the kitchen staff know she was up and to bring her coffee while she settled back into the pillows.

It was one of her favorite songs by a band called the Ozones. They'd only just made it big the year the world went to hell so she was a little surprised to hear it on there, but she'd had it on her old player so it shouldn't be a surprise really. They'd been massive, after all. She started to scroll through the songs on the player, much more expensive than hers had been.

"This is my memory card!" she said softly, but out loud. "He must have put it in here."

She dug around the covers until she found the piece of folded paper. Maybe it was a note.

"If you carried this thing around for all these years, the music on it must mean a lot to you. I really like some of it. Have a good day, my sweet."

Her heart melted a little at that. She'd promised herself she'd stop comparing Rex and Rager, but damn, sometimes it was hard not to. Rex wouldn't even share his MP3 player with her. Rager had found her a brand new one and had put her SD card inside of it. It was old technology, but she had loved stuff like that when she was a teenager and she still did, she found as she went to answer the knock at the door and took the tray from the servant there.

She got back in bed, sipped at her coffee, and then ate her pancakes with a happy smile as Janis Joplin sang about life with a fella named Bobby McGee. It was a song her mom loved, and she'd learned to love it too. Rager had given her this moment of happiness, he didn't have to, but he was an observant fellow, and he'd wanted to make her smile. He'd more than done that.

When her breakfast was done, she went into the bathroom and ran hot water into the tub. She used some of the soap she'd found in an abandoned store to make coconut-scented bubbles, and then stepped into the soothing water. Music filled her ears as she leaned her head back against the edge of the large tub.

Rager had told her that one day, everything that was old now would be made again. Things like soap, razor blades, all of it would be made again. One day. For now, they were still having to make do in many ways. She wasn't going to complain a bit. She wasn't one of the wolves, she wasn't a servant. Sometimes she watched them, saw how they rarely smiled, how many walked around with their shoulders bent, and wished she could do more to help them.

Rex had said the most terrible thing to her, that he hoped she died giving birth. He thought she was a traitor to their kind. But she wasn't his kind anymore, she reminded herself as she let water fall between her fingers. She lived a life of privilege that she couldn't have imagined a few years ago. Even a few months ago, she'd have said this was impossible.

Sure, she and her little band of a family might have been able to find this house, they could have made do in it, but how would they power it? Would they have even made it this far? Many of the wolves had turned into cannibals, they'd started to eat non-wolves, which wasn't quite cannibalism. Or was it? Ann wasn't sure, but she knew it was close enough that it made the world dangerous.

The aliens put those wolves to death, and left only those that had never intentionally, murderously, tasted human blood. Now, those that had survived were virtually slaves. She hated to think about it, she didn't want to think about it, but she did. The same way she thought about the words Rex had spit at her.

Guilt plagued her, she'd been so in love with Rex for most of her life, but even before the aliens came she'd started to question that love. She'd given him so much devotion, and all he'd ever shown her was disdain. As if her loyalty was owed him for being a high school sports star and nothing more.

Now that she thought about it, he hadn't lifted a finger to save any of them, not even his parents. It was her father that did that. Not Rex, the homegrown hero. The hero of nothing. Not like Rager, either.

Rager had crossed galaxies, universes with his people, and then, they'd started to save what was left of life on Earth. With their advanced technology and science, they were recreating the world. With the help of the humans and the wolves left, they had started to bring the world back to life mechanically as well. Power plants were operating again, and she'd heard that there would be a medical center opening soon.

Which reminded her that her mother had tripped over... nothing. Something? She wasn't exactly sure what had happened that made her mother smack her head like that, but she decided she'd call later to check on her. Her mother had never been a clumsy woman and that trip had left a nasty gash on her head.

The water started to cool, but instead of getting out, Ann ran a little more. It was decadent, indulgent, but her thighs were sore. Which made her remember her mate and what he'd done the night before. In so many different ways. Her body was covered in his marks, bruises from fingers that clenched a little too hard for an earthling, the love bites his lips left on her thighs, the scratches from his nails along her back. It all needed to be soothed.

The hot water swirled along her body as it mixed with the cool and she sighed in bliss. She wouldn't complain about her new life, how could she? She just wished everyone had the same privileges. It wasn't fair that Amanda and Stephan Wolfson were servants while Ann and her parents lived in what was now luxury.

Her father worked for his privilege, she knew that, but her and her mother? It was almost like being in the 19th century again. She and her mother were the ladies of the manor, posh and privileged. In reality, they were just ordinary people that managed to survive the end of the world, or the near end of it.

With a frown, she sat up, put her MP3 player a safe distance from the edge of the tub, and started to clean up. She'd have to figure out a way to make this all right. Okay, so the aliens didn't want the wolves mixing their DNA with the humans. For a moment, she wondered if it was only racism that caused that kind of thought. But then she thought about those wolves that had killed non-wolves.

Maybe it wasn't racism.

There was only a fraction of a difference between her DNA and Rager's, enough to ensure they weren't related and enough to know they were different. His eyes were orange, after all, that wasn't really a color that showed up in the Earth population. All of the aliens were huge men, more like the Nordic people than her own. Tall, broad, and fully muscled, they were all made for battle and hard work.

Earth didn't need to be a battle zone, though, she thought as she ran a sponge over her legs. Rex had talked about a resistance movement. She could understand that the wolves wanted to change their fate, nobody wanted to be enslaved, but did it have to come to the war Rex seemed to crave?

There'd been a hungry gleam in his eyes every time he'd talked about fighting the aliens. It had made her wonder about his sanity, that gleam, and the way he talked. Surely, he'd noticed how little effort it took to conquer their world? Rager and his merry band of aliens had basically waltzed in, sat down, and declared themselves the rulers of this world, because they *could*.

Even if Rex and his cronies managed to take over a military base, they wouldn't be able to defeat people that could basically *fold* time. That's how Rager had explained it, as a kind of folding of time until the travel time was shortened because all of the extra space had been removed. When he'd explained it, the whole thing made perfect sense. She wasn't sure anyone on Earth would be able to build the kind of technology it would take to be able to do that, but it made sense to her. In theory.

With a final rinse from the handheld showerhead finished, Ann stepped out of the tub and wrapped herself in a huge towel. She smoothed some coconut oil into her skin and dried her hair before she put on a white linen dress. It was light and sleeveless, with a row of buttons down to her knees. It would get her through the day.

She picked up her phone, the only thing she could think to call the device, and went downstairs to the kitchen. She talked with the cook about what they would have for dinner and then went out to the garden. She saw her animals out in the fields and smiled. Soon, things would almost be back to normal.

But this was a fresh start. Did they really want normal? The old normal? With all of the political bullshit and families torn apart over things that didn't really matter in the grand scheme of things? Did they want all of that hate and anger back?

She sat down on a bench and watched as the gardeners went about their duties. There were imaginary lines here, in this new world, lines that she didn't like. Lines between wolves and non-wolves, aliens and humans. Wasn't that enough?

She knew there could never be utopia, people were far too flawed even when they thought they were perfect. But couldn't they create a world that was close?

Rager and his soldiers came here looking to expand their own world, to have more room to grow. Did they have to follow the rules of that world? Couldn't they break some of those old laws that kept them tied to ways that had never worked?

Throughout history men had tried, over and over, to force people to bow to a new way. To their way. Those ways had succeeded for a time, sometimes, but empires had fallen, time after time. With a sigh, Ann plucked one of the flowers from the white jasmine bush at her side and smelled it. Couldn't life be this simple? Take what you need, give something back, and just let people be happy?

The problem was with people like Rex. Douchecanoe Rex. What an absolute shit, she finally decided as she got up to head into the house to get out of the heat. Her love for him had been a childish thing, something that only a child could feel. She hadn't understood what a grown woman could feel, how much she could feel. She might have been naïve, stupid even, but she'd come to know that grown-up love was different.

Rager was a man, there was no doubt about that. A very skilled man, that took his time, that made sure she was right there with him at every stage. Whether it was in bed, or out of it, he asked her opinion, he made sure she was on the same page as him. Except for the whole wolf thing. That was different.

Did she love him, she wondered as she went into the library to find a book to take back up to bed with her? Her fingers played over rows and rows of leather-bound books, old books that might have fetched a small fortune back in the old world. She didn't even notice them. Her thoughts were on his smile, the way it sometimes revealed a crooked molar in the back of his mouth, on the right upper side. And the way he'd look at her when his thoughts turned to... other things.

He could burn her up with those eyes, if she hadn't already melted into a puddle. She hadn't known any of this was possible, that you could become so fascinated with pleasure with someone, that you could be almost... *addicted* to a person. Was that love? Or really only addiction?

She didn't know, and she didn't really have anyone she could talk to here about it. Amanda and her mother would probably listen, but it would be awkward. She wasn't really sociable enough to know the other female mates in their area. She'd met them, spoken to them, but she'd always been distracted, her thoughts tangled up with Rex in the early days, or with Rager now.

She pulled out a more modern-looking book, with a dust jacket, and drifted back up the stairs to their bedroom. Her phone buzzed and she pulled out an earbud to answer it.

"Hello?"

"Hello, sweet Ann. How are you?" His voice purred into her ear, a sensation that she'd only experienced with him.

"I'm a very happy woman, thank you. I love your

gift." She leaned back against their bedroom door as she spoke, a new smile on her face. "It's perfect, really."

"I'm glad you like it. I thought it must be important to you."

"It is. Music is one escape I've missed terribly, and you've given it back to me. It's perfect, really."

"Good. I only want to make you smile."

"You do, don't doubt that for a minute." Since their wedding night, it had been like this. He'd made the world rock for her all over again, and since then, well, she felt a bond forming unlike any other she had, and sometimes there were awkward silences, but not often.

Now, if only she could find a way to make sure the rest of what was left of this world got to smile too.

3

"The league is meeting again tonight. Rex wants me to make sandwiches. Like his silly group is some women's luncheon or something, and I'm his personal cook. I told him I wouldn't. He can do it himself if he wants to." Amanda's voice stopped Ann as she walked toward her mother's kitchen the next day.

"Good for you. He really needs to just… stop!" Her mother's voice, in the same hushed tones as Amanda's, kept her still against the wall.

Ann wasn't sure why she hid against the wall and listened, but something told her to wait.

"I know. This isn't the way to change things. It's just so stupid, and I'm afraid." Amanda's voice broke on a hushed sob and Ann couldn't just stand there anymore.

"Hi, I'm here," she called, guilt all over her face, she could feel it.

"Oh, hi, honey." Mary looked at Ann, her own face flushed with guilt, and Amanda turned her face away from them both. She saw the other woman was chopping onions so she could blame the sob and the tears on that, but Ann knew it wasn't that at all. And they didn't want her to know.

Ann's heart twisted in her chest as she realized the two most important women in the world to her didn't trust her. Why, she wondered as she sat down and started to shell peas from their pods? Was it because Rager was her mate? Or was it because of how Rex had treated her? Surely, they didn't think she would use his activities against him in some stupid idea of revenge. She wasn't that kind of person, and never had been.

"What's up, ladies?" Ann asked, and looked at each in turn. They shared a glance and put on pleasant smiles.

"Nothing, baby, just ladies talking. How are you?" Her mother came over to her and stroked Ann's hair. "You look good."

Mary sat down beside Amanda and started to chop tomatoes, her head down, where Ann couldn't see the expression on her face.

"Thanks. I had a good night's sleep." They'd had to go to a surprise dinner with one of the other villages' leaders. Mayors as they'd chosen to call themselves. They'd left when other people started to leave, and by the time they'd traveled back to their house, it had been after midnight.

Rager had gone straight to sleep, and she'd slept in a little late. Which meant there'd been no playtime, something that hadn't escaped her notice. Even now her body wanted to go to him, despite the fact that she'd just sat down at her mother's. It was some internal craving, something that she'd started to think she'd never be able to control.

She reminded herself that she needed to stay for a while, Rager wouldn't be home from work for a while anyway.

"Are there any problems?" Ann prompted, but both women focused only on the jobs they were doing. "You know you can trust me, don't you? I'm no different just because the Supreme Overlord is my mate."

"Everything is fine, honey, I promise," Amanda said with a confident smile as she looked up at last. Ann could see still a red tinge around Amanda's eyes, but the tears were gone. Not the onions then.

"I hope so. If there is trouble, I'd like to help, you know?" Ann looked right at Amanda, but the older woman's head was down again, on the onions she still chopped at.

"How are things at your house, Ann?" Mary asked, and Ann turned her head to look at her mom.

"Fine, Mom, though our peas aren't this nice." She held up a pod and then shelled it. "I'll have to get some of yours."

"Of course, baby, you brought me those lovely tomato plants, you can have all the peas you want."

"Thanks." It felt too much like small-talk and Ann cringed a little. This wasn't how today was supposed to be. "How's your head?"

Mary's blond bangs covered the cut on her forehead, but Ann noticed how she shook her head to make sure. Mary had on a sapphire blue, long-sleeved blouse, but the sleeves were rolled up to her elbows. Paired with black jeans, it wasn't exactly the kind of outfit one might expect from a mayor's wife, but Mary had always been practical, not flamboyant.

"I've heard the other wives of mayors want to institute some kind of uniform for us all. Have you heard anything about it, Mom?" Ann had overheard one of the wives talking about it the night before.

"No, can't say that I have. What an utterly ridiculous idea. Why on Earth would they want to do that?" Mary looked at her daughter with obvious confusion.

"To make sure… ahem, to make sure that *others* know their, well, their places." Ann felt ashamed to say anything like that in front of Amanda, but she knew the woman wouldn't think bad of her. Amanda had on a black utilitarian house-dress, something a maid might wear, but she'd chosen that as a practicality. She'd been used to lab coats in their old life, her house dress wasn't that different to her. She'd even said it was kind of reassuring, familiar even.

"That is just nonsense! I hope you put her in her place." Mary looked at Ann expectantly.

"I'm still new to all of this, Mom, it's…" Ann's voice faltered as she looked for the right word, "intimidating sometimes. I don't know how much power I have, what's right or not, what's expected of me, nothing."

"Honey, you're the mate of the Supreme Overlord of Earth. I don't know in the world of their business, but here, in our midst, you have control of all of the women. Did Rager not make that clear to you? It's one of the stipulations your father asked for. Rager was more than happy to agree. You'll even be over any alien women that might come over."

"What? Why didn't anyone tell me? I really need a copy of that agreement thing they brokered between themselves." This news changed things a little, and she'd definitely make sure to speak up about this stupid uniform idea. They were not going to become some kind of hermit nation, with coded uniforms and bowing. For fuck's sake, it all made her head throb. She winced and rubbed at her temples, the pain a surge that came up from behind her ear and straight into her temple.

"Are you alright?" Mary asked quickly and leaned over the table to look at Ann.

"Fine, just a headache." Sometimes, like now, she was reminded that her father had been forced to basically trade her to the alien leader. Normally, she put it in the back of her mind and got on with life.

At the moment she was clearly reminded that's exactly what had happened. How long would it continue, this arrangement where Earth women were forced to mate to alien men? Would there be alien women here eventually, or would they stay on their planet? That faraway place that Earth people couldn't pronounce?

"I'll get you some aspirin, Ann." Mary went to stand up, but she plopped back down immediately. "Maybe we all need to go into a cooler room for a bit. My head is spinning."

"Mom? What's wrong with you?"

"It's just the heat in here, baby, don't worry."

More of that brushing things off garbage. Ann sighed and rolled her eyes. "I'll get the aspirin, Mom, you stay there."

"I'll get her a glass of cold water. You sit right there, Mary."

"Fine, but I'm alright. I don't know why you two are fussing so much." Mary's voice faded away as Ann walked back to the downstairs bathroom. There'd be aspirin in there.

Mary's color had come back to normal and her eyes were clear when Ann came back, two small aspirin in hand.

"I poured you a glass of water too, Ann." Amanda pointed at it when Ann sat down.

"Thanks." She looked at the two women, her eyes narrowed. "Now, which one of you is going to start telling me some truth?"

"Don't you take that tone with us!" Mary rebuked; her eyes narrowed. "I'm still your mother."

"Fine." Fat lot of good that did. She'd tried though. "Keep your secrets. I'm going to head home, I think. My head is not getting any better, and you two are driving me nuts with your secrets."

"Oh, Ann, they're not secrets, baby. It's just, well, there are some things we need to work out first, figure out completely. Then we'll talk to you about them, I promise."

"You'd better. I'm the Supreme Overlord's wife and stuff." The words came out weakly, more rueful than anything. "Not that it does me any good."

Amanda and Mary both laughed and stood up to hug

Ann. The transporter was outside and she headed to that, her booted feet a loud clomp against the ground. She'd dressed for scavenging in black combat pants, heavy, steel-toed leather boots, and a black t-shirt. She probably shouldn't be seen out scavenging, but she liked doing it.

Every layer of dust and dirt that she removed to reveal diamond rings or teething rings for babies, revealed a layer of history. This was who they used to be, who they wanted to be again. Ann hid any jewelry or valuables she found in an old camera shop close to her home. Nobody would be looking there for a while, she thought, and she didn't want women like the ones at the party last night to have the silly things either.

They were very pretty rocks, but still rocks. Women like the ones that had suggested the uniforms, and those that had quickly agreed with her, would covet those rocks, would cause trouble for things like that. It was better to just keep them out of the way. They could find their own if they wanted them that desperately.

Ann headed towards a section of town she hadn't explored before, there was a spice store there at one point and she wanted to explore it. Most of the spices would probably have gone stale by now, but there might be some seeds, like celery seeds or dill seeds, that she could plant. The seeds might produce plants, or might not, it was worth a shot. Both would be good plants for pickling vegetables, once they'd produced some proper vinegar.

She'd scoured a library until she found a book on how to make vinegar, pickles, and quite a few other ways to preserve food. She wanted to make sure there was enough, even if the winters did prove to be milder. If they turned out to be colder, that preserved food might prove useful.

That, and she really missed pickles.

She landed the transporter and hopped out, her headache already forgotten. With swift feet, she moved into the building through the empty doorway and made her way inside. The sun was still up so she could see just fine as she walked through the shop. There were six rows, and each one had different spices from around the world. Some of the cheaper items were in plastic bags and long discolored. They were too dry to do anything more than give off the memory of a smell, she found when she opened one.

There were some smaller metal cylinders and Ann's eyes went wide when she saw them. She opened one to test it, and the smell of curry powder was prominent and so fresh that Ann's eyes went round with pleasure. Oh, these might just be worth taking.

She loaded up the backpack she'd carried in with her, curry powder, chili powder, and a variety of others, all went into her bag. When that was full, she went to the front of the store. There were some reusable canvas bags there and she filled two more of those with spices, and then thought about it. She filled three more bags, to take to her mother, and started to load them all into her transporter.

She'd found cylinders of the seeds she wanted and hoped they would all prove to be just as well preserved as the powders. It took one more trip before she had all of the things she wanted for now loaded and she settled back into her driver's seat. A quick stop at her mother's house to drop the spices off and then she'd head home.

Something caught her eye as she started the transporter. A beam of sunlight that reflected off something as the sun started to go down. She put her hand over her eyes to shield them and squinted at the wall. A wolf's head covered the side of the small building, with glowing yellow eyes that gave off waves of menace. The artist had done a good job of painting a rather fierce-looking wolf, but what did it mean? Was it a threat? A territory tag maybe? Like the gangs used to have?

She wanted to tell Rager about it, but she didn't want to cause trouble for the wolves. She stared at the painting, lost in the sensation of being trapped between two worlds. Amanda, Stephan, and Rex had been a part of her life for as long as she could remember. They'd become family during their time in the bunker. But she was the supreme leader's mate. Shouldn't she tell him?

This all came down to loyalty, and just then, she felt as if she'd been ripped in two, one side with her old world and the other with the new world. She turned the transporter off and sat there, too overcome with emotion to move. Which side was she on?

Her body said it was all about Rager, it didn't care what she thought. She wanted him, no matter what. Even now, torn in two, she wanted to go to him, to curl up into his arms, to feel his touch make the world disappear for her. Her mind told her body to shut the fuck up, and at this moment, it won.

Her head said she had to use her status to protect her family, all of them, and her body could dig out a vibrator from any of the shops she'd already raided. A vibrator didn't have a heartbeat, though, or a voice that rumbled over her skin like a touch in its own right. A vibrator couldn't touch her in all the right spots with wet kisses or fingers that knew just the right pressure to make her breath catch in her throat as endorphins flooded into her veins. It couldn't make her feel like the most important, most beautiful woman in the world. Or the most cherished either.

Because it wasn't just sex with Rager, there was more to the whole thing, it was that modalla thing that Agnar, the man that had made them mates, had spoken about. Their spirits were joined in a way she hadn't quite wanted to face yet. She didn't feel him as a touch along her spinal cord now, not like she had during their mating ritual, but she was always aware of him. And that was the worst thing of all, right now. She knew, no matter how much one part of her wanted to, she could never betray her mate. Not even for her family, she'd tear out her own soul if she did.

4

———————————

*A*nn stretched in bed the next morning and was surprised when she found Rager was still beside her. She turned to look at him, concerned that he might be ill. They'd been mated for almost a month now and the only day he'd taken off was their mating day. And that had only been a half-day.

She looked at him, still asleep, and relaxed. His jaw was lined with bristles of dark hair, and his face looked… somehow soft. As if sleep took away some of his gruffness. It wasn't that he was less attractive, far from it, he just looked far more approachable. She tentatively put her hand on his jaw, to check for a fever.

He was always warm when he was asleep, so she wasn't sure how she would tell, but he didn't feel any different than he normally did. The moment she touched him, those odd, bright orange eyes of his opened.

He said something, something she couldn't understand, and her brow furrowed. "Pardon?"

"Sorry, it's my language. Good morning, Ann." His smile was lazy, relaxed, pleased even. He pulled her to him, tight and close. "I love waking up to you."

"I think I like it too. But, why are you here?" She tilted her head into the pillow and he closed his eyes as he ran a hand down her body.

"I am leaving my second in command in charge for two days. We're going exploring, my love."

"Are we now?" A happy question. Exploring sounded nice. Like it was time away from the weirdness here, and adventurous.

"We are, yes. Now, if you'll please get off of me, I might be able to drag myself into the shower before I ravish you."

"Oh, ravish me? Now, that's a term I've never actually heard anyone use." She slid from the bed but didn't push her nightgown down over her hips. She sent him a look over her shoulder, a sultry one she hoped. "But if you'd like to do that, I'll get back in bed?"

She paused and waited for his answer. He just turned over and groaned, as if frustrated beyond words.

"Noooooooooooooo. We need to do this. And I'd like you to come with me. I don't want to leave you here for two days. I'd hate every minute of it." He got out of the bed and headed to his bathroom without another word.

"Well then…" she laughed and went to her own bathroom. Thirty minutes later they were dressed, fed, and ready to go.

"Where are we going?" she asked him as the transporter started. It was his transporter and much faster than hers, with sleek lines on the black metal. She'd thought it was black paint, but it wasn't.

"Up north, maybe up to Canada, I'm not sure yet. It depends on what we find on our way up."

"What's to the east of us?" She asked as the vehicle began to move and rose into the air.

"There's a deep break in the land, you're lucky California didn't just disappear into the sea. Then, there are places where people survived, we're picking them up as fast as we can and bringing them to us. Others are going to a town we're building up in Ontario."

"Oh, you're building another town?" She hadn't known about that.

"Yes, we don't want to keep all our eggs in one basket, I believe is your saying?"

"Yes, it is. Good idea. Maybe we can visit there one day? I never got to travel much, Mom and Dad were always working when I was a kid, and then *that* happened." She waved her hand at the landscape. "I didn't really get to see much of the world."

"You are young, aren't you? I sometimes forget. You seem so… mature for a young Earth woman."

"I had to grow up quickly, didn't I?"

"I suppose so. How old are you, Ann?"

"You mean you don't know, Rager?" She looked at him, surprised.

"No, I don't. I know your people age more quickly than mine do, but I really don't know. All I wanted to know was that you were of a legal Earth age to marry, or mate as we call it, and that was all really."

"Oh, I see. I'm 20."

"That young?" He saw her appalled look and quickly spoke again. "Not that I think you look older, it's just you seem so… calm, I guess is the right word. Like an older woman would be."

"That young," she said, her lips tight against her teeth as she glared at him. "How old are you then, if your people age slower?"

She'd thought he was around 30, and while they'd never actually spoken about it, and she'd just given him grief about not knowing how old she was, she was guilty of the same.

"I'm 48, Ann. Old enough to be your father!" He howled with laughter, but she just gaped at him.

"Seriously?" Her eyes scanned for the signs of age, gray hair or lines around his eyes and mouth, but there were none, just smooth, youthful skin, healthy and clean. "Fuck."

"I'm an old man in your world. In mine, I'm no older than you really. Well, a little older, but not by much."

"Fuck." She could only stare at him. "You're really 48?"

"I am, Ann. Does it bother you?"

"No, I just can't believe you're that old."

"Oh, now who's doing the insulting?" He smiled at her to let her know it was said in jest and looked out. "You might want to start looking around now. There might be people trying to get out our attention, or run from it."

"Why do you capture people that don't want to come with you?" It was something that had bothered her from the first contact she'd had with the aliens.

"Because, sometimes, people fear the unknown, and obviously we are unknown. As you know yourself, we're not here to harm any of you. Just repopulate the planet and bring it back to life."

"I see," she said softly, her eyes on his face. He didn't look like he was rehearsing a speech, or speaking from rote, just an honest statement that made it easier for her to sit there with him. "That's why we tried to hide from you. That and we'd heard you were killing the wolves."

"Only the bad ones." He spoke softly, his eyes on what was around them too. Most of the landscape was empty, but here and there were dots of houses or buildings. Some were in good shape, but most were just shells of what had once been. It was sad, to see it all from up here. Down on the ground, the scale of it all was immense, but up here, where you could see how much had really been destroyed, it made her speechless.

"It's so sad." Ann finally broke the silence. "There used to be so much in the world, but now? It's just so sad."

"Not for the planet, or the other lives here. The ocean life, the wildlife on land. Even the plants and rocks are better off without man crowding the planet."

"You're right. Just before the cataclysm, I read an article online that said most countries were using up a year's worth of supplies in less than five months. Some barely lasted two. It was unsustainable. Even if the cataclysm hadn't happened, something would have broken sooner or later, and we'd have all been at war for goods or dying of diseases."

"That's truer than you know, Ann. We came here before, as I've said, a very long time ago. We left a few of our species here. We thought they'd interact with the local populations and maybe make their own colonies. We had no idea they'd breed with the people you call Neanderthals and populate the entire planet."

"Bred like wild rabbits, did they?" She knew they had, but she'd wanted to lighten the mood more than anything.

"Yes, as you well know. There were 8.5 billion people on your planet when the cataclysm happened. That's, well, it's outrageous, really."

"How so? Isn't your planet overcrowded?" Her look of confusion was hard to hide. Hadn't he said that at some point before?

"Not really, we only have 1 billion people on a planet of the same size. The last time your planet had only that many people was before the 20th century. In the 1800s. We're also far more technologically advanced and we did all of that without the troubles and wars that your planet has faced."

"How? You don't have enough people..." her words trailed off as he shook his head.

"We use our resources more wisely, don't engage in warfare like your people do, and value science above all other things. We missed a lot of what your planet had." He was being delicate, she could tell, and she let him sidestep the issue he was avoiding. There was one major difference here, his people didn't have a religion. Her planet had hundreds, if not more.

"I know what you're saying." She could understand it much better now. His people had been focused on science, and a way of life that made life better, not on subjugation and suppressing science.

"There's a lake over there, and a little cove of trees.

Shall we stop there? I had some food and clothes packed for us. We'll be gone a couple of days, there's bedding too if we have to stay in the transporter for shelter. And a tent."

"Did you bring the kitchen sink too?" She asked with a laugh as he set the transporter down.

"No, but I thought about it." He grinned and turned the machine off. "Let's see what's down there, shall we?"

"I'd like that." She got out and walked around with him to a spot where the grass was short and not too far from the water's edge. There was a nice little beach that would make it perfect. "It's a lovely spot."

"Not as lovely as you, Ann." He said it as he spread a blanket down on the ground and sat down on it. There was a basket with food that had been tucked away in a cabinet, and a bottle of wine as well as one of water.

They ate homemade pimento cheese sandwiches, some fresh vegetables, and had a glass of wine as the sun rose higher in the sky. The day warmed up, and even the shorts and t-shirt that Ann had on were almost too much clothing. "I think I might go for a paddle around the lake."

"You aren't going to wait for the allotted hour?" he asked, his smirk in place.

"Just how much television did you watch before you came here?" She was amused at the amount of knowledge he had about her world, but it was hard to picture him sitting still long enough to watch that much television.

"Hours. Weeks. Years maybe? I don't know, sometimes it felt like an eternity." He said it ironically, his eyes full of amusement. "It was interesting, what can I say?"

"I can't see why. We basically committed mass suicide. Even before the cataclysm."

"True, but the way you got to it was fascinating. All of that horror and for what? Nothing, really."

"I'm not sure everyone would see it that way, Rager, but some would. And how come you're a soldier if your planet is so serene?" The question had occurred to her earlier, but she'd waited to ask it.

"There are other planets around us, filled with other species, and some the same as ours. Not all of them developed as we did. Some went a similar path to yours and want to invade the other planets nearby. That's part of the reason we're here, so far from our own world. If we can settle here, we might just leave them to their wars and come over here for the peace we wanted."

"You might find it hard to take it all." She knew it was a silly statement, but it was as close as she could come to a warning without betraying what she knew.

"Oh, there is dissent, and will be more I assume. ? They will either come to heel, or they'll find life won't be so pleasant for them. We won't have war in our new world."

His voice was harder when he spoke, with a note of warning to it. She knew it was dangerous ground they were on, but she had to tread it. "I would tend to agree with you, Rager. I don't see the point in going on as we had been. It will only lead to the same thing again, won't it?"

"It will. But you and your family are safe, don't doubt that." His eyes bored into hers, and she knew he was telling her far more than that. She wasn't sure he knew about Rex, but she suspected he might.

"Thank you. I'm going to get naked now if you'd care to join me?" She gave him a saucy wink and stood up. Her clothes came off as she headed to the lake, abandoned in the grass. Then she had a thought and turned back to him, her arms over her breasts. "You all didn't resurrect ticks did you?"

"Ticks? Those tiny, blood-sucking horrors? No, we didn't. No fleas either."

"Thank fuck for that. Last one in is a rotten egg!" She screamed the last with a laugh and ran into the water. Then she ran right back out. "That's fucking freezing!"

She stared at him, shocked at the coldness.

"It's coming out of the mountains, of course it is. Come on, I dare you." He ran past her, his own clothes thrown away, and dove into the water.

"How can he stand it?" She stuck her right big toe in the water and backed off. "Nope, not freezing my tits off today, buddy."

She went back to the blanket, her clothes in her hands, salvaged from the grass. She looked over when she heard splashing and saw him treading water, happy as a seal. "How the hell can you stand that?"

"Our bodies are different. It doesn't feel cold to me." He swam out of the water, very obviously not cold.

Her eyes went straight to a part of him that was very, very warm, in fact. "I think I can see that. Want me to take care of that for you?"

"I thought you'd never ask." He dropped down beside of her, his lips fused to hers with a hunger that she knew would never go away.

5

His fingers played across her cheek as he kissed her, a sweet distraction from the sensual slide of his tongue along hers. With a long press of his lips against hers, the supreme leader of the alien overlords pulled back, just enough to look deep into her eyes.

"You are amazing in so many ways, Ann. I didn't know you'd be this perfect, even when I dreamed about you." His voice was low, but she heard him.

A slight smile pressed her lips up, but he kissed her again to stop her from speaking. "Leave the clothes off."

Ann let her head fall back, a laugh of delight the only sound she made as his lips played down her neck. Fingers stroked the silky skin down along her chest until both hands kept a breast. Each tip was teased into a hard peak with his fingers before his mouth came down to circle each one in liquid heat.

"Mm, that's so good," she murmured but she wasn't really paying attention to anything but the sensation of his lips as they sucked at her nipple. Her hips pressed into him, his body between her legs. He was just as naked and ready as she was, but neither was in a rush. They rarely had so much time together that they wanted to just use it as wisely as they could now.

Her fingers came up to his head, slid into the thick pelt of his dark hair, and she allowed herself to do nothing else but feel and then feel some more. He drove her mad with his touch, but it was a madness she happily embraced. Two months ago she hadn't known this man really existed. She'd started to dream about him, but she hadn't known he was real. Now she did, and the soft press of his fingers into her flesh was something she knew, but she still craved it.

That touch reassured her, it made her feel safe, but it also set her on fire.

Rager had taught her many things since their mating, things about sex and the adult body, but the most important might have been to take what she wanted, to demand it even. His attention was on her left breast, so she soothed the ache for attention the other had with her own hand.

She hadn't counted on him noticing, or on him

moving his head to suck at the nipple through the two fingers she pinched it in. She squeezed a little harder as his tongue stroked over the tip, and wasn't surprised when her hips jutted up against him. The pressure of his leg down there, so tight against her, fired an instinct to move, to seek solace wherever it came.

"You're going to break me too soon, angel," he whispered raggedly when she moaned deep in her throat.

"Then fuck me, Rager. Make the ache stop."

"I want to taste you, to stroke you, Ann. I want…" but she pulled his head up to hers and shut him up with her lips, and her tongue. She kissed him with so much uncaged passion that it broke his own will.

They both cried out with satisfaction when he shifted his hips and sank into her wet heat. He was so deep inside of her that he couldn't sink any further. With a satisfied hum, he turned them over and pushed her up against his raised legs. "Let me at least look at you as you use my body for your own needs."

She smirked happily but didn't say anything else. She let her head fall back, her hair free and loose now, down her back. It teased at his thighs, but she knew he wouldn't complain. Instead, he urged her to move, pushed up into her to start the dance that only he would ever see her dance. There was nobody else in this world she'd ever want as much as she wanted him.

"Tell me it'll always be like this?" she asked him, and he nodded his head, in total agreement.

"Nothing will ever take you from me, Ann, and now that we are mated, we'll never want another person. Not unless one of us dies, and I'm not going to let that happen."

She reached for his hands and their fingers clasped together as she found just the right pace, for them both. They moved together, perfectly in time, as they drove higher, to the place that only existed for them, between them.

Ann gasped when the explosion came, deep inside of her, and she heard the hiss of Rager's inhaled breath as she clenched around him. Her back arched, and she drove herself down onto this thick length until she couldn't breath and the world was darkness that slithered with the coils of pleasure.

He followed her, his own cry filled the air around them, but neither cared. There likely wasn't anyone around to witness what happened anyway. She sank down onto his broad chest when it was over, her body wrung completely dry. She was exhausted and wanted nothing more than to languish in his arms for the rest of the day.

Rager had other ideas. The minute he caught his breath he stood up, fetched his clothes, and got dressed. "Come on, lazy bones, let's get back to our task."

"Do we have to?" she whined from behind the edge of the blanket she'd pulled over her nudity.

"Yes, we do. Come on now. Let's get this done, then we can stop again when the sun goes down."

The transporters produced their own power, somehow, and they wouldn't need fuel. Rager's was much better than hers, and she knew they could watch movies, prepare food, and do quite a lot more if they needed to. It was almost an RV and an airplane mixed into one vehicle. "Can we watch a movie in the transporter later?"

"If you want. I've got some bedding stowed away, and if we leave it running we can keep the air cool and any nasty bugs out. Or we can pitch a tent."

Only, their version of tents were basically minirooms that expanded from a pack that was only two feet square. She'd seen them used before, to act as temporary rooms when the invaders were going to be away from their ship for a while and hadn't been assigned quarters down here yet.

"That could be interesting." She put her black leather boots back on, and stood up, fully dressed now. Her black combat pants and black t-shirt were now almost a uniform when she wasn't going to some function or lounging around the house.

"We'll decide later then. Ready? I love those pants on

you, by the way. They make your ass look like a peach that needs to be bitten into."

"That's not sexist at all," she snarked, but grinned. She'd actually loved the compliment. When he smacked said ass, she glared but had to admit, she liked that part too.

"It's mine, and I'm glad you keep it in such nice shape." He kissed her as they settled back into their seats.

She didn't run anymore, she used a treadmill in their home, and tried to maintain a pace that would mean she could walk for hours if she needed to. That fear of being out in the world, of having to walk far distances, hadn't left her, and she liked to keep fit, anyway.

They both went quiet as they flew over the tall hill that had sheltered them and found a small city on the other side. It was flattened, nothing left, and no hint of mankind was in sight.

"It's so sad," she whispered, not for the first time that day.

"I know, baby. I'm sorry. Do you want to take a nap?" His concerned eyes scanned her face, but she refused to be so soft.

"No, I'd like to know what we're really facing. I'm not a child. I can do this."

They flew on for a few more hours but the world here was empty. There were no signs of life, despite the disappearance of the ice. There were no tent cities, no clothes blowing on clotheslines, no fires, nothing that she might have hoped for.

They flew up the western coast of what had once been the United States but was now just more real estate for the invading aliens. Would they all end up speaking the same language, with the title of earthling as the only thing that separated them? Ann didn't think that was necessarily a bad thing, it was about time the people of the planet realized they were all riding the same rock through space, but she did wonder how many of them were left.

"How many have you found so far, in this part of the world?" she asked as he steered them through the air. The sun had started to go down and he turned on the navigation lights, but there were no headlights. They wouldn't really work this far up. There were landing lights, but they didn't need them right now.

"A few thousand so far. We've only really looked around southern California and the section to the south that belonged to Mexico. We found more people down there than up here. It was cold there too, but not as bad. We'll find more though, you people are resourceful and there was time to prepare. The really bad snows didn't start for a few months, so we're hoping to find more."

"I hope you do." She'd often wondered who would survive, what kind of people they would be. Would they be bad people that took advantage of others to stay alive, or would they be the good kind of people?

"Don't worry, we won't allow criminals into the places we're setting up. They'll be taken to a separate place. Where they can feed off of each other if that's what they choose. We keep it all under control there, too, though." He gave her a reassuring look and drove on.

Ann scanned the darkness below for signs of life, lights, fires, anything that might mean another human being existed out there. There was only darkness, though, and she was glad when Rager finally set them down for the night.

They had a meal of hot pinto beans, cornbread that had been kept hot in a special bag, and a salad. An odd dinner, but a part of their daily diet now. There weren't enough animals to have a solely carnivorous diet so they were forced to rely on other means of nutrition. None of them complained, they just took what they were given.

The spices she'd brought home had made a lot of the food far more delightful than it would have been. Even now, she could taste a hint of chili powder in the beans and smiled. That taste was there because of her, she thought with a sense of pride. She wasn't completely useless, at least.

"What do you want to watch?" Rager asked as he put

their empty dishes and the bag back into the cubicle they'd been in. "And should we set up the tent?"

"I think I'd like to set the tent up." It wouldn't take long, they just had to undo a strap and the tent would do the rest. There would even be a bed and a door once it was all set up. She was thinking about the fact that they'd have to go out of the transporter to go to the bathroom and the process for opening the hatch on that was more complicated than setting up and taking down the tent.

"That's cool. I'll bring in the video viewer and we can still watch a movie if you want."

"That sounds good." She went off for a minute on her own and looked around. They were on top of a mountain, covered with trees now, and she needed a place to ease her bladder. She found a spot and did her business. When she stood up, she saw the face of a woman through the trees. She gasped as she did her pants back up and stared at the woman. "Who are you?"

"Please. Don't tell him you saw me. I have a husband, children, in a bunker not far away. I came out to get fresh water from the stream over there." She pointed to somewhere behind Ann and deeper into the trees. "We don't want to go with the aliens. We just want to be left in peace. Please, don't tell him you saw me."

The woman looked clean, healthy, and perfectly capable of making up her own mind about how her life went. Ann understood the sense of Rager's words, but she could see the fear on the woman's face and the way she glanced behind her shoulder, as if her entire world lived just beyond where she could see. Ann decided to not say anything to Rager. Let one family have a little more time on their own, before their world turned upside down.

"I won't tell him. We'll be gone tomorrow, so when you get back, stay down there until at least mid-afternoon, okay?" Ann held her hands out flat, palms down, in a motion meant to keep the woman from feeling threatened. "How did you know about them?"

"We have a radio. And my husband's seen a few of those plane things they have. Thank you, miss. You'll never know how much I appreciate it." The woman melted away then, into the trees and back to her life.

Ann stood there, guilt a rat that gnawed at her brain. She should tell him, but she remembered the fear, the terror, of being captured by the aliens not so long ago. They weren't allowed to decide where they went, or what they did. They were told. And that still irked Ann. They were treated like cattle, even if that treatment was humane. Surely, people should be allowed to decide?

She had a feeling the aliens would find the family, eventually, but for now, they were living in their own happy world. Ann decided to let them have that for a while longer. She walked into the tent-room and closed the door behind her. It was twelve feet square and had an inflatable bed, a small inflatable couch, and recessed lights that were battery operated but still produced a good deal of light. A small podium to the left side of the bed served as a table and a nightstand.

Rager had set up the video viewer on it, basically a 15-inch tablet, and had one open and loaded when she crawled into bed, naked, to curl around him. The covers were soft and heavenly and smelled of her favorite fabric softener. "Lets just lay here together, shall we?"

"Are you alright?" His arm curled around her shoulders and pulled her tight to him. She felt his warm mouth on her forehead and smiled.

"Yeah, I'm just tired. I need quiet for a little while. To be here with you and quiet, that's all."

6

"I really don't see why you're objecting to the uniforms, Ann. They're *dogs*, after all. Human dogs." The woman's shrill voice, at the height of condescension, filled the study of Ann's home two days later.

Ann closed her eyes for a minute and tried to wipe the look of scorn off of her face. "Penelope, you're very stupid, do you know that?"

The room filled with ten other women, the mates of other aliens down the rank line that stretched out behind Rager, gasped as one. Normally, they all ignored Ann because she didn't say a lot. When she did speak, the women usually just blinked and then ignored her. She'd had enough of it and refused to let Penelope lead the group, as she usually did, anymore.

"How dare you?" Penelope, dressed in a mint-green

silk suit stood up on tacky white pumps and glared down at Ann. "I'm…"

"Nobody compared to me, Penelope. Sit down and shut the fuck up." Ann stood up from the chair she was sat in and looked around the room. "I'd like to remind you all exactly who I am. I am the supreme leader's wife. None of you will ever, ever outrank me."

She wasn't happy to do this, but after an hour of listening to their petty ideas and plans, she'd had enough. "The wolf-shifters are not subhumans. They are, actually, stronger than us. They are healthier than us and likely to outlive us all. These stupid ideas that we have to treat them like slaves have to go, and I will tell you right now, I will not have this idiotic idea of *uniforms* spreading any further. I hate uniforms, I refuse to wear one, I don't care how much time you've spent on the design for the mates of the aliens, Penelope. It's an ugly idea. And the uniforms you've designed for the wolves are, frankly, atrocious. Sit down and don't stand back up unless I tell you to."

She looked around the room, now firmly in her control, and hoped none of them could see how surprised she was that any of them had actually listened to her. She felt a shaking inside, like she might fall down, but she stood firm. She had this one chance now, to make the world different from the way it used to be. She was going to take it.

"We will not be having these cute little meetings anymore, ladies, where we only talk about which of us is pregnant, or what new treasure we've found for our houses. We are the mates of the leaders of this new world, and it's time to act like it. We're going to start talking about schools for the children we plan to produce, about making sure all children in the world get an education, and how we can help our mates turn this into the kind of world they came from. I don't know if any of you noticed it or not, but the world we lost? It wasn't working, and well, the aliens are lightyears ahead of us. Literally."

Ann looked around, saw a few pouting faces, but not many. She saw that most of the women looked relieved. Some realness, at last, she could see it in their expressions, mixed with that relief. "Now, anybody have any other ideas?"

"As you said, Ann," a woman with red hair stood up and said, Ann thought her name was Meg but couldn't remember for sure, "we've all been discussing babies and pregnancies, but where are we going to have those babies? We have no hospitals now, or clinics even. I was a nurse before this all happened, and I think we need to talk with our mates about what kind of healthcare we're going to receive from them. If we need to make a clinic, you know?"

"Totally agree. Want to start a committee on that?"

Ann nodded with approval. This was much better than listening to Penelope droning on about color schemes and what wolves were allowed and not allowed to wear.

"I gather textbooks when I come across them, and non-fiction books too. I've kind of started a library in a building behind our house," another woman said quickly, her dark brown eyes alight with joy. "If anyone wants to use my books, I'll be glad to show them to you."

"That's really great. What else can we do, ladies? It's time to stop waiting on our mates to do things and start thinking for ourselves, a little bit."

The room filled with excited chatter and Ann felt her own relief, at last. She might have overstepped her bounds, telling them all that the wolf shifters were stronger and all of that, but it was the truth. Even Rager had said they were. They were a threat to the purity of the DNA here, though, and that was the only reason they were being kept at a lower rank. Since they'd come back from their trip, they'd talked a lot more, and he came home earlier in the day than he used to.

They'd even broached the subject of the forced servitude of the wolves. It hadn't exactly been a calm discussion, but Rager had listened. He didn't see it as slavery, but Ann did. She thought she'd started to make some inroads on that front, and was hopeful, at least. Now, she'd taken control of these vapid meetings these women insisted on having, maybe she could make some more progress.

She'd sat through most of these luncheons wondering how these women had survived. They were even looking for a nail technician, who could do their nails for them! Ann had a lot of worries on her mind, and today had been the day that it all broke. While she'd hated to lose her temper, she could see now that maybe it was what had been needed. The women were excited as they talked about all of the things that would move their lives forward in positive ways.

Later, once everything was rebuilt and life started to move forward, they could discuss things like what to replace hairspray with, and getting their nails done, but right now, they needed to work on far more important things. Ann was glad to see that had begun.

It was hard for her to trust people, the situation was too new, too out of the realm of possibilities. Her mind wasn't made up about what was safe and what wasn't. Not even Rager had situated himself into a box yet. Ann's body was certainly addicted to the man, but her mind still wondered.

She'd wanted to love the man she married, mated in this case, and the idea of an arranged marriage would have horrified her when she first fell for Rex. It had horrified her, up until the moment their modallas were merged. Then, everything had changed. She wouldn't exactly call what she felt for him love yet, but it was bordering on severe infatuation. Given time to learn to trust him, she might. Maybe. He was still an overlord.

Ann decided to get a glass of juice and walked over to the table where a servant stood waiting to take orders for drinks. "May I have some apple juice, please?"

"Certainly, ma'am." The young woman kept her eyes down and even did a little bob up and down. Ann frowned and looked back at the women behind her.

This was exactly what she didn't want. Rager told her that his world advanced because they'd taken a totally different path to the one the people of Earth took. This was an old path, and one that hadn't worked. "Do you need a break?"

"What, ma'am?" The woman looked up, startled at the question. Humans didn't often ask her questions like that, Ann had to assume.

"Are you tired? Do you need a break? We can have someone else serve drinks if you are."

"No, ma'am. I'm fine, honest." The young woman with curly, dark hair and bright blue eyes looked worried, her eyes on Ann's for only a second before she looked down again. "I'm a good worker, I promise."

"Where were you before you came here?" Ann asked as the woman handed her a glass of juice with ice in it.

"At Ms. Penelope's, ma'am." Ann didn't think it was possible, but the woman's head sank even lower.

"I see." Ann glanced at the woman in question and wondered what she could do about that woman. "Well, you don't have to call me ma'am, and you certainly don't have to curtsy, please don't do that anymore."

"Yes, ma-, er,..." her voice trailed off. Confusion and panic warred on her face and Ann realized that was her fault.

"Just call me Ann. What's your name?"

"Robin. Do you want anything else?" Ann could see she was frightened and decided it was time to back off. For now.

"That's all, Robin, thank you."

"You're welcome." A tiny hint of a smile appeared, but then disappeared but Ann saw it before she turned away. It wasn't hard to be nice, after all.

"Ladies, I have another appointment after this, so if we can start wrapping up the conversations, I'd appreciate it," Ann called out as she headed towards the door. Another hint that it was time for them to get the fuck out. She didn't want to be rude, but she could tell now that she had to be direct, or they'd ignore her.

Her head had started to pound, and she just wanted to be in Rager's arms for a minute. She didn't really have another appointment, she just wanted them to all go away. As if she'd conjured him, her mate appeared at her elbow and pulled her out of the room.

None of the women saw him, and none seemed to

notice that she'd disappeared. They'd basically ignored her dismissal, too caught up in new ideas and the beginnings of plans to get up yet, so Ann let him pull her out of the room and down a dark hallway. It led to a storage area that was rarely used, so it was dark, quiet, and cool. His lips found hers as he pressed her gently against the wall.

She felt every inch of him pressed up against her, and still on the high of finally taking control, she pulled him tighter to her, kissed him with far more desperation than she normally did. She was so hungry for him. The sweet taste of whiskey on his tongue, the sensual feel of his hands as they roamed her body, all of it, and she didn't protest for a moment when he lifted her against the wall, with her own red dress now around her hips, and tore her underwear away.

"You're going to end up with sycophants, you know that, don't you?" he purred into her ear as he pulled away just enough to undo his pants.

She wanted to reply but he slid into her before she could. All that came out was a moan, and then his mouth was on hers again and she didn't care. All she knew was the feel of him, the ragged sound of his breath as he drove into her, and the way it felt to have him slide inside her.

It was quick, but oh so satisfying, the way he drove into her. Even the punishing clench of his fingers on her ass felt good, and she whispered his name against his lips. He pulled away, to kiss her just below her ear as her fingers started to clench on his shoulders.

She concentrated on the way he pressed into her clit as he thrust into her, on the exotic smell of his skin, and what it felt like to bite down into his neck as the first wave crashed over her. He grunted when her teeth nearly broke the skin, but he didn't protest. He seemed to like it, and that was a new, heady thought to her. So much power in one single day.

And then he hit something inside of her, some spot that only he had ever touched, and the world became only them. His touch, his sound, his smell, his taste, and the sensations that came with each of them. There was only pleasure and the strangled sound of his own release.

When it was over, when she'd slid down the wall, patted the skirt of her dress back into place, and removed what was left of her underwear, she looked up into his face. He was so much taller than her that she had to crane her neck back to see him. His lips came down to rest on her forehead, and he breathed her name.

It had started as a dirty and very passionate escape, and now, for the first time, there was something… more. There was an intense look in his eyes when he pulled back, and she felt the echo of it in her own. "Rager?"

"I'm proud of you, Ann. You took control today, and you've started to lead the women in a new direction. You made me... proud."

He looked as if he'd wanted to use another word, or to say something more, but he pulled away. She reached for him, but he moved to the side.

"I have to get back to work. You did really well. I'll see you this evening."

She watched as he walked away, and tried to get her hair back into the bun she'd tied it up in. He had started to care for her, she hoped, and if she'd made him proud, well, maybe she should trust him?

She went back to find that the women had all started to leave and she told them all goodbye, even the terrible Penelope. When she closed the door on the last one, she leaned back against it, a smile in place. It wasn't the best thing to do, to insult a woman like Penelope, but she'd done it, and taken her rightful spot in the meeting. Luncheon, whatever. She pushed away from the door and strode up the stairs, ready for some music, and to make a few plans.

For a minute, just for a minute, Ann wished the old world was back. Yeah, she had high hopes that the world would be better, and she planned to work hard to do that, but she missed things like Pinterest and Google. It would be nice to order something from Amazon again, or even Ebay. Now, she had to take what was brought to her or go and scavenge for it.

There'd been rumblings about problems in the sector that she often hunted for finds in, and now she had to bring a guard with her when she went out. She stared at him for a moment, the back of his head covered in a helmet that gleamed dark blue in the sunlight. She didn't like it one bit.

She turned and walked through the aisles of what had once been a furniture store, the contents now were mostly destroyed, but sometimes she'd find hidden treasures. So far, she'd found a lamp in the shape of a tree with prisms that dangled from small limbs. She wasn't sure where she'd put it, but she'd find a place.

Once she was certain she was done with the place for the day, she turned and started toward the doors. The sound of booted feet as they marched on the road outside stopped her. She looked back at her guard and wondered what to do. She didn't want to talk to a bunch of soldiers right now, so she pretended she was interested in some curtain ties that had molded into a mess a long time ago.

She knew they'd probably only stopped for a break, so she waited and moved down close to the door to look at some Christmas decorations that had lost most of their paint. It was a holiday of the past, one that she might resurrect, she decided. She moved closer to the door as she walked by each row of decorations, all hung up on a pegboard that barely clung to life.

She went still as she heard two of the soldiers come close to the door and glanced at her guard. He didn't look concerned, just bored, and waited patiently. He stepped a little closer when she turned, but voices stopped them both. Rager had quickly made it a rule that all of the aliens had to speak English when they were not on board their ship. It still hovered in the sky, almost big enough to block out the sunlight as the sun made its way across the sky. Because of this, the ship moved every day, not far, but enough to make sure all of the gardens had enough sunlight.

"I heard Rager's human bitch is out here somewhere. He shouldn't have mated to her. We need pure blood."

Ann felt ice water run through her veins. Not this shit again. She glanced back at the soldier that guarded her and knew he'd heard it too.

"You really need to shut up about that, Melno. Somebody will hear you. Then we'll both be fucked."

"I don't give a fuck who hears me. Rager has dishonored us all by marrying that human. Her DNA isn't as strong as ours, it's not as *good* as ours. She's nothing but an inferior breeder. We'll have women of our kind here soon enough; he should have waited."

Ann felt rage replace the ice, and she looked at the soldier again. He was recording everything that was being said.

"Our men and women bred with the humans here before, Melno. You know we're virtually the same. The difference in our DNA is so minute you can barely tell the difference. Why has it got such a huge bug up your ass that he mated to her?"

"It's dishonorable. He shouldn't mix our genetics with them, any more than any of us should mix with those wolf-people. Creepy fuckers, all of them."

"They aren't creepy, any of them, you moron. Come

on, let's get back in formation before you get us into trouble."

"I'll need you two to stay right there." Ann looked back as her guard spoke up and walked past her.

"Shit, I told you, Melno!" the other one whined, but the happy chatter didn't say much of anything.

Ann didn't know the ranks of the alien soldiers, but she knew her guard outranked most of the foot soldiers. He called their superior over and for the next two hours, she sat in the furniture store and wished she'd just walked away from the soldiers. Then she wouldn't have heard that man and she would have been home by now.

There'd been a lot of whispered conversations, questions from the leader of the squad on patrol, and then, a lot of nothing happened. She was told to stay put, so that's what she did. She waited, on a recliner that she covered with a blanket she'd found wrapped in plastic. The blanket and chair both smelled moldy, but it was a place to sit.

"Are you alright, Ann?" Rager's voice came from behind the chair.

"Oh, I'm fine. It was just some asshole running his mouth. Can we go home now?" She was tired, dirty, and hungry. All she wanted to do was go home.

"Of course. Let's get you out of here." He kissed her dirt-streaked forehead, and they left the building. She climbed into her transporter and followed him home. It was a quick trip, and she was in the shower before too long. He sat outside the glass cubicle, and talked to her about what had happened.

"Nothing really happened, Rager. The guy just said some things about how I was inferior and that alien women were coming soon, and you should have mated with one of those."

"I don't want any of those women. I wanted you before I even saw you, Ann. It happens like that sometimes. Not for everyone, but true mates have that ability."

"So you don't want some tall, buxom alien woman instead of me?" She rinsed the shampoo from her hair and waited for his answer.

"No, although, in our world, we can have more than one mate. I don't want another mate, though. Just you."

"Another mate? You mean polygamy?" She was surprised, but not completely shocked.

"Yes, men and women can take more than one mate, if it's agreed upon by all involved, in our world."

"Oh. Women can have more than one mate?" Her voice was steady, but she was still surprised.

"Of course, why not?"

"It's just, well, not the usual way here." She scrubbed off the rest of the dirt and sweat from her body and turned off the taps. "We usually only mate with one person down here. At a time, at least. People get divorced or break up, then move on, but normally, it's one person at a time."

"Except for the people that had lovers on the side," he responded, a chuckle in his voice.

She looked at him as she toweled herself dry, her head tilted. "Try it and I'll break your legs."

"Try what?" He put on an innocent look and blinked at her.

"That whole mistress thing," she said with a smile of her own, a very sweet one that didn't match the look in her eye. That look said she might be playing but she meant it. "I'm not that kind and…"

"Neither am I, you feisty little monkey. Calm down." He pulled her into his arms and pulled her close. The towel fell off, but it didn't matter. She was in his arms.

The day dropped away as he kissed her in a way that told her there never would be anyone else that he could kiss like that. She blinked when he pulled away, surprised that he'd stopped.

"You need food and so do I. Oh, that man will be prosecuted, by the way, and probably sent back to our home world. I refuse to have someone like that on our planet and what he said cast doubt on me, not just you. My family leads our home planet, and that's my role here, to do the same."

"What will happen to him?" Ann asked as she went through the door to their bedroom. She pulled a silky gold nightgown from the wardrobe and a robe that matched. She slid her arms into the short sleeves and tied it at the waist.

"I don't know, he may be sent to one of the other planets, or maybe imprisoned. We don't imprison people often, we try to put them in places where they won't cause problems and can adjust to life. He's obviously not suited for this planet."

He wouldn't meet her eyes, instead, he turned away and opened the bedroom door. She followed him on bare feet. Most of the servants would be in their own quarters now, or out with their friends and family. Only the kitchen staff would see her and they were all women, so she didn't care that she was in her nightclothes.

"I guess we can drop it then." She was glad the man would soon be gone, the tone of his voice hadn't necessarily frightened her, but she hadn't liked it. What if he'd decided to do something about it, or had started others thinking the same way? It could cause problems for them all.

Rager wasn't the only one that took a human mate. Some of those beneath him had, and other soldiers had as well. This was the second time something like that had happened, and she had a feeling it wouldn't be the last. She'd have to be vigilant and listen more carefully from now on.

What a mess, she decided as she sat down at the dining room table. His men didn't want him mated to her, and the wolves wanted to be the rulers of this new world. They seemed to have forgotten it was the aliens that cleaned the place up, not them. It was the aliens that had made it possible for them to all live outside of their bunkers and shelters. It was ridiculous that the wolves thought they should be the leaders now.

Ann finished her dinner quietly, and then she went up to bed to read a book. She put her music on and read for a little while, but the events of the day and her worries played on her mind. She couldn't settle into the book, and she'd read two chapters without having any memory of what she'd read.

She decided she'd go see her mother tomorrow. Although, that brought its own stress. Her mother still seemed off, somehow, not her normal self, and she and Amanda did a lot of whispering now. It bothered her that they still didn't seem to trust her, or thought she shouldn't know something.

What were they hiding? Was it about Rex? Was he causing more trouble with his ramblings about wolf superiority?

She was so keyed up that by the time Rager came up to bed, she had turned off her music, put down her book, and stared up at the ceiling blankly.

"What's on your mind, Ann?" he asked as he dropped

his clothes and slid into bed.

"Nothing, really. Everything. So much has happened in the world, it's hard to take it all in sometimes."

"I know, sweetheart. You were very young when this all happened. But old enough to have formed an idea of what you wanted your future to be. It must have been terrifying for you when the world started to rumble and tilt."

"It wasn't fun, but it could have been worse, I guess. I still don't know the full extent of what happened. Do you all know?"

"We are forming theories about it. A lot of it had to do with plate tectonics, but some of it was caused by man."

"How so?" She turned her head to him and waited.

"All of the fracking, the drilling, you all but turned your planet into a sponge with all of your mining and construction. It's full of holes, and empty spaces that used to be full of minerals and rocks. All of that was a sign of the mess it's been turned into."

"I'm going to have to think about that one for a little while." She turned away, her eyes on the ceiling again. "It makes sense, and it was something I wondered about, but there was no proof, you know?"

"Well, from what we've seen, and put together, it makes sense. I haven't been given the final report yet, so we'll see what it says."

"That sounds like a plan. Do you want to watch a movie?"

"I don't. I'd like to just lie here and appreciate my mate, if that's alright with you?"

"That sounds like a good idea to me." She turned into his arm, put her right leg over his and her head on his chest. Safe again, that was the first thought to come. Peace was the second. He put his hand on her leg, to hold it in place, and squeezed her thigh gently.

"This is nice," he said softly above her head.

"What?" she asked, her cheek pressed into his chest.

"This, being here with you."

"Why do you sound surprised?"

"I've never done it before you. I've been to bed with women before, but I've never cared enough about one to keep her in my bed."

"You care about me?" she asked it very carefully, as if it wouldn't matter if he said no, to give him that escape. This was still new to them both, and they'd only been together for less than two months.

"I do, Ann. Which is why I will do all that I can to keep you safe. I swear that to you." He kissed the top of her head and she put her right arm over his chest, to cup the place over where his heart was.

"I'm glad you do, Rager." She didn't know what to say other than that. *I care about you too* just seemed trite. She wasn't ready to say love, but she did care. She turned her head enough to kiss his chest, and settled down a little more into the bed. She'd taken her robe off, and now it was just the silky feel of her nightgown and her skin between them.

The night was warm, but the house was just cool enough that the covers weren't too much. With a deep sigh, she closed her eyes, and just relaxed against him. She was happy she realized. Peaceful and happy. She thought about his smile, the way his eyes caught hers sometimes, and passed along a message without words. He'd tell her he was happy with a wink, or that he wanted her naked beneath him with a hot look. She had come to know him well in a short time.

She even knew his parents were back on his home planet, that he had a brother and a sister, but he wasn't in a rush to go back to his own world to see them. He was dedicated to this project, to repopulating Earth with people from all over the universe. He was also looking for a cure to the wolf situation. That still hadn't been explained, but who knew what had been released from the depths of the planet during the cataclysm?

They'd all learned one thing the day the whole thing started; anything was possible, and wolf-shifters were hardly a surprise at all. Now, if they could all just learn to reach for a common cause, that would really be perfection.

$\mathscr{A}$nn ignored the sounds of giggles behind her as she headed for her homeroom class. There was a new rumor going around about her crush on Rex, and she was about to die from the shame of it all. She rolled her eyes as she walked into the classroom and stared at the gigglers as they walked in behind her and whispered comments to each other. It didn't help that they all stared right at her as they whispered.

With a huff and swish of her hair, she sat down at her desk, the one she'd been assigned at the beginning of the year. The idiot gigglers were behind her, at least she didn't have to face them from up here.

She wasn't an overly proud girl, but this was high school, even if Jason Mamoa was their teacher. How he managed to act in Hollywood movies and teach was beyond her, but whatever, right? They had the hottest teacher in the nation. Despite his hotness, and the fact that she normally didn't care about high school bullshit, being laughed at still stung, even if her brain said they were only silly teenagers and to ignore them.

She wanted to start reading her schoolbooks, but they had somehow become glued to the ceiling and she stared up at the flapping pages with extreme confusion. How the hell had that happened, exactly? She turned her head, but still couldn't figure it out.

With a start, she realized that she was now the teacher, and five rows of students stared up at her. Wait, how had that happened? She was confused again. But then, she remembered she was mated to Rager and nobody could hurt her ever again. She loved him and that was all that mattered.

Suddenly, she was alone in their kitchen, the staff all gone, just her and the joy that came with preparing a meal. She made dinner for them both, set out a bottle of wine, and decided that it was time they had some fun.

A gentle hum of appreciation from behind her let her know Rager had come in to join her, at last.

He came up behind her, wrapped his arms around her waist to pull her close, and kissed her neck.

"You not only look good, my love, you smell good too!" His face was buried in her hair, as he inhaled her scent.

Dinner was forgotten as his hands reached out to

turn her around to face him. She followed his guidance and let him take control. His kiss was deep and aroused, accompanied by a moan from Ann as he pushed her up against the countertop. Her legs wrapped around his waist to draw him closer.

"I love you." His words were whispered against her neck, a brush of silk that tickled her in just the right way. The touch made her gasp, the words made her heart skip a beat.

"I love you too, Rager." She pressed his head to her neck but he surprised her by pulling her away from the counter.

CARRYING HER TO THE BEDROOM, he put her down on the bed, stripping down before sliding up beside her.

"You're lovely in your silk nightgown, my love, but I have to get you out of it. It's not very useful when I only want to feel your skin."

Ann grinned at him and threw the gown away, somewhere across the room.

"And where would you like to kiss me first?" She spread out on the bed and looked up into his eyes. There were some weird disco lights going now, but she ignored them.

"Right here, I think." He pressed the tip of his tongue softly to her chin before he sucked at her skin with his lips. "Oh yes, that was a very nice place to start."

She giggled and waited to find out where he'd go next.

He hummed, but continued to move his lips around her body before he circled back to her breasts.

"And here, of course," he whispered as he gave each tip a very good dose of attention.

Ann watched him with her breath held, her heart beat so frantically she was sure it would explode. It was just a game, just him and his playful side, but sex with Rager always ended up being so much more than… just sex.

Rager cheated by going back to each nipple a few more times until Ann wanted to scream at him to fuck her. She wanted him inside of her more than anything else, the ache that filled her, the need, about to break and overfill her as he licked and sucked the tender flesh of her peaks.

When his free hand slid down her stomach, down to spread her folds, she finally couldn't hold back the need and she screamed as her body went taut.

"Rager, oh please, I'll die, please, don't stop."

She encouraged him to send her even higher, the sweet torment of the rasp of his tongue against her sensitive nipples only added to her desperation, her pleasure.

"You're going to wake up the entire house if you aren't quiet," he laughed softly, and that's when she became aware that she wasn't dreaming anymore. Rager really was over her, his lips around her nipple as he teased her clit with exquisite precision.

She tried to smother her moans, and to keep the sound of her begging quiet. But she soon gave it up as her pleas turned into demands that he give her what she needed the most.

"Let it go, Ann, show me what you can feel."

Ann gasped when her body bowed into a tight curve as the tension deep inside of her exploded into waves of brain-bending pulses of pleasure. She breathed in deep to draw in a reserve of air as she blew apart.

She wanted him to be inside her, to find that place of completion together with him, to ride that wave that she balanced on only when he was inside her.

Because he was the only one she loved. He was her mate, her one and only, and she needed him. She gave in to the desire of her heart and her body as she pulled him down to her. She didn't ask this time, she demanded he give himself to her. To take her with him.

He did the only thing he could do for her when she was so insistent. He slid inside her tight heat, sinking in deep to her slick depths before he bottomed out.

This was her nirvana, she thought, the only place where she truly belonged. With him.

Their pace quickened, their breath became ragged, and their skin slick. She bit into his shoulder as he found that spot all over again. He gave a cry of surprised pleasure as he began to lose control. For a moment, Ann wasn't certain this was real, maybe it was all a dream. But she'd worry about the whole thing later.

She knew only pleasure right now. Later she'd worry about whether she'd said I love you to him for real, or if it was part of the dream she'd woken up from.

When he rolled away from her, and she was calm at last, she began to wonder. He must have touched her in her sleep. He must have started to tease her at some point when she was asleep, and that had changed the whole direction the dream had taken. She didn't think she'd told him she loved him for real. It wasn't time for things like that. Not yet.

She sat up and looked over at him. She could see him in the soft light from a small lamp over the bed. His dark hair was tangled sensually, a testament to how much her fingers had pulled at it. And his eyes were two bright orange orbs, filled with nothing but pleased happiness.

"I'm going to take a shower, want to join me?"

"I do, but no more playtime. You woke me up moaning my name, and I figured if you were dreaming about me, I might as well fulfill your dreams for you." He kissed her shoulder as he followed her into the bathroom. "But I have to be up early in the morning, so no more shenanigans after this."

"Tease," she whispered loudly, but turned the water on in the shower without complaint. They cleaned up, but by the time the soap was rinsed away, the need to touch each other was back.

She decided to give him a gift of her own, and sank down to her knees. He was already aroused, thick and long, proud even. She took his length in her hand and began to do her best to swallow all of him. It was impossible, at least right now. She'd learn to take him all if that was what he wanted, but for now, he was happy with what she gave.

He leaned back into the hot spray of the shower, a moan his only answer to her attention. His head fell back on the tiles, and his eyes closed, she saw when she glanced up at him. The hot hardness of his cock was all she needed to guide her, and she followed the pulses that came with each slide of her tongue over the head and the jerks that each slip of her wet mouth down his length caused. His body told her what he wanted more than his mouth or eyes did. He wanted the tight suck she lingered over as she explored the tip more with her tongue, the sucking vacuum of her lips around him. Her hand stroked the thick length until his hips began to move, and he fucked her hand and her mouth.

She didn't want him to hold back, she wanted to get

him off quick and dirty. Not because she wanted the task over but because it felt good to make him lose control, to make him come in her mouth and hand. She felt like she was in control, knew she was in control, and that for once, the Supreme Leader of New Earth was little more than a puppet in her...mouth.

She smothered a giggle and went back to work. His fingers closed on her head, and he grunted out a command. "Hold still."

Even now, that command wasn't a command but a defeat. He couldn't control himself, and it only made the satisfaction deep inside even stronger for her. She looked up into his eyes as he began to thrust his hips, her eyes full of her own pride and delight. There was also a dare there, to completely let go. All he had to do was let go, and he'd find relief as he came in her mouth.

"Fuck, I can't...." But she knew what he couldn't do as she felt the first pulse of his release. "I can't resist those eyes, Ann. Fuck."

She moaned around his cock as he let his head fall back, but his hips didn't stop, not for quite a few seconds. She held onto him with her hand, but he still set the pace, until she'd swallowed every drop of him, and he'd sunk back against the wall. With a playful smile, she stood up, and stepped out of the shower. She turned back to turn the hot water off, and he looked up at her.

"You're going to kill me." He didn't exactly look like that was a bad thing.

"You'll die happy, then, won't you?"

"I suppose I will, Ann." They climbed back into bed once they'd dried off and he put on some pajama pants, and she slid on a cotton nightgown.

Cuddled up together, she turned to her side, tucked right up against him happily. Her body was sore, tired, but satisfied. He fell asleep before her, but she didn't mind. She loved being there with him, so close and warm. This was what married life was supposed to be like.

Maybe one day they'd not only say they loved each other, but they would actually be in love. She was fascinated with him, and she cared about him, but did she really know what love was? She thought about her parents, how they'd always worked together to provide for her, to make sure they were all safe.

They hadn't argued a lot, and if they did, they hid it behind closed doors. There were never any arguments in front of Ann. Disagreements, perhaps, but never all-out arguments. She wasn't silly enough to think they'd never argued, she just knew they'd thought of Ann before anything and protected her from it. She hadn't argued with Rager, but then, she wasn't totally trustful of her position in his life yet to argue much.

She was learning, though, that she could talk to him

about matters that concerned her. She was slowly introducing the idea that the wolves needed to be treated better. She was also coming to see that the people of Earth had a lot to learn from the aliens. If the people here were willing to let go of old ideas, old ways, the new world could be the miraculous place they'd all dreamed of for so long.

If they weren't afraid to work, and listened to the new way of thinking that Rager and his people brought with them, war could be a thing of the past, and people could live if not in some kind of hippy, flower-power commune of love, then in peace and something like harmony. Ann wanted that so much, even if it was a lofty ideal to reach for. Utopia would never be possible, she knew that, but maybe they could get close to it.

She shifted a little, to ease the ache in her left knee. She had a lot to do the next day, but her brain wouldn't shut up. Thoughts and plans for schools, a new clinic, and other advances filled her head. These ideas mixed with her brain suddenly reminding her of things she needed to get done. *You have to see your mother tomorrow, you have to go to that meeting, there's a kitchen mixer at that store that you haven't gone back to yet.* On and on it went, until she sighed with frustration and reached for her music.

That was the one thing that could soothe her, distract her enough to help her get to sleep. Tomorrow would be busy, and she needed to sleep. She'd had her fun time with the man that was her mate, now she needed to rest.

She put on some Fleetwood Mac and just as Stevie started to sing her into sleep, her brain decided to mess with her one more time. *What if you're pregnant?*

She groaned and turned on her back. The ceiling was dark, and for a moment, she couldn't decide if her eyes were open or shut. She blinked just to see, and decided they were open. What was wrong with her?

Maybe you're pregnant.

This time it came with her mother's voice, not her own. Not that her mom had ever nagged her, but she could just hear her mother now. She wouldn't know for another week and a half, and even then, she could only suspect. She wasn't sure, even though she'd had the same health and sex ed classes as the rest of the girls in her school.

If it had been two weeks since her last period, then they could have conceived a child, it was certainly possible. Had she actually had one since she'd been married though? Now that she thought about it, she wasn't exactly sure. Maybe she had it all wrong?

Anxiety was eating her alive, and finally, she got out of bed and went to the door. Maybe a walk would help. She didn't bother with the robe because she knew everyone would be in bed at this time. It was the middle of the night by now.

She walked through the house, down to the kitchen, and out of the back door. She could see the moon, high in the sky, and the cow made a low noise of hello. It must have heard the back door close. With a sigh, she turned to her flowers, and brushed her fingers along soft petals. Her heart started to calm and her mind slowed down.

She saw a light in the garden shed, and walked towards it on bare feet. She could hear voices inside, but not what they said. She made out one word, fight, and then another, ours. What were they talking about in her garden shed?

It must be the wolves, there wouldn't be anyone else here at this time of night. She tried to hear more, but the people inside started to move and the door handle clicked. She pressed herself against the wall on the side, where she'd be hidden in darkness, and held her breath. She had a feeling none of those inside would want her to know they were holding meetings in her shed, and wouldn't react nicely if they saw her.

9

"*W*hat's going on over there?" Ann asked a few days later.

"Joana is pregnant," Meg, the nurse that had spoken at the last meeting, told her.

Ann glanced in the direction of the woman named Joana, and saw Penelope doing her damnedest to ingratiate herself to the woman. Penelope might turn out to be a problem, but for now, the meetings had a focus at least.

"Thanks, Meg. Have you checked her out?" Ann knew it wasn't really any of her business, but she was curious, and wanted to make sure the woman was taken care of.

"Yes, and your husband sent a few men out to help me with the clinic. I'll have it open soon." Meg's brown eyes were filled with excitement and Ann was happy about that.

"That's good news. I still think the aliens have some technology that could be of use to us, though. I'll talk to Rager about it."

"That would be great. I wasn't hinting, by the way, just letting you know." The woman looked away, as if worried, so Ann put a friendly hand on her arm and smiled at her.

"I know, Meg. Don't worry." She stepped back from the small group of women she'd been chatting with as Meg's face relaxed.

"Thanks, Ann."

"Let's get down to business."

There was a podium set up in the front of the living room, her headquarters for now, and she went to stand in front of it.

"Good afternoon, ladies. I'm happy to report that a lot has changed over the last few days. Instead of discussing the best kind of potato salad, and what baby names we should pick out, we've now got a library started thanks to this kind lady." Ann paused to point at the woman in question, and waited for the applause to die down. "And Meg has just told me we'll have a clinic soon. We're making progress, good progress."

More applause and Ann looked around the room. She knew the faces but some of the names still escaped her. She decided she'd have to sit down and memorize them at some point. A new face caught her eye and she made a mental note to introduce herself to the woman. She was pretty, with black hair and tanned skin. It wasn't the prettiness that caught her attention, however, it was the startling lightness of the woman's blue eyes. Ann nodded at her and then continued.

Nope, no other new faces. Time to ask questions, then. She now had an agenda for these meetings and a plan of how each one was to go. Deviations could happen, but she wanted to stick to the plan she had if it was at all possible.

"Now, does anyone have suggestions about what we should do next?" Ann waited but the women just looked at her blankly.

It reminded her of a few nights ago when she'd hidden at the side of the shed as the men inside filed out. Each one of the eight men had walked out with the exact same blankness on their faces. She'd managed to get back to her bedroom and cursed herself for going out. She'd wanted to get some air to help her sleep and had gone to bed with more worries.

She'd told Rager about the meeting, but he hadn't said anything else about it since then. The meeting must not have been as sinister as she thought if Rager hadn't said anything more about it, and the fact that these women wore the same expression as those men was only coincidence, she told herself. With a minute shake of herself, Ann began to speak again.

"I suggest some of you that don't have projects yet get into groups and try to find something to do that can keep you busy. What resources do we need that we don't have yet? Will we need daycares, maybe? Or pre-schools? I know we'll need teachers eventually, perhaps some of you can look into what courses teachers had and start training some people in those fields." Ann leaned against the podium, her elbows were flat against it, and she could see she had their attention now.

"I know some of you may not like it, but I do know a wolf shifter that used to be a science teacher. She's a cook now, but she was one of the best science teachers around, and she would be a valuable person to speak to." The women started to shift around and murmur, so she held her hands up and stepped back a little. "I'm not saying we put her in charge of the children, I'm saying we should talk to her about the process of teaching. Get some ideas from her."

That calmed them down and she smiled as she started to relax too.

"Now, does anyone else want to speak?" Ann could see Penelope wanted to but didn't dare put her arm up. Good, she could sit down there and keep her vileness to herself. "If that's all then, I'd like to end this part of the meeting."

Nobody protested so she walked away from the podium to the place where sandwiches and some tea had been set out. She'd found quite a few large cans of powdered tea. It wasn't the greatest flavored drink in the world, but it was cold and tasted of something besides water.

She saw that the women had started to form into work groups, although Penelope's little group of three seemed to be disinterested in doing anything at all. They just stood around and watched the rest of the women as they tittered behind their hands. Ann decided they'd either find something to do or they would become outcasts. The new Earth had no room for people that only wanted to stand around idle while they gossiped.

She saw the new woman over with Meg's newly formed group. There were four women with her, all eager to talk to Meg. Ann went to them and listened as Meg spoke.

"I can't train you to be nurses, but I can train you to be as near to one as I can. It will take time and dedication." Meg looked at each woman sternly and they happily nodded.

The new woman spoke up then.

"Hi, I'm Skye. I was still in my second year of an RN when the cataclysm happened. I might be able to help. I didn't get to get my degree, but in my spare time, I studied as much as I could. I raided the local bookstore for my course books and went through every single one I could get my hands on. I just don't have any practical skills, obviously. I was on my own, so…"

Her voice trailed off as she saw that she had everyone's attention. Her cheeks turned a dusky pink and she looked away.

"That sounds magnificent, Skye," Meg said, her voice soft. "Right now, you're probably as well prepared as you can be. And you can teach the others too. Thanks for stepping up."

"I agree with Meg," Ann said as soon as Meg finished. "You're just as valuable. You can learn the hands-on stuff as you go along. It's not exactly the best practice, I guess, but we have to take what we can get, don't we?"

"Yes, it sounds like you're well ahead of us, anyway," another woman in her 30s with blond hair and happy green eyes said. She was a tall woman and competent looking. "I worked as a paralegal, but that's not going to do us much good now, is it?"

"It might, one day," Ann said quickly, more to reassure the woman than anything. The aliens had their own rules and laws and none of the Earthlings knew for sure what all of them were.

She made a few more mental notes and walked around the other groups until she'd spoken with everyone. Except Penelope and her little group.

"Hello, Penelope," Ann said quietly as she walked up behind the other woman.

"Ann… I…" Penelope looked uncertainly around the room, anywhere but at Ann. "We're, um, we've decided we're going to work on daycare and providing nannies to the other wives."

"Have you now?" Ann asked without inflection. She wanted to see how Penelope responded.

Ann stood there and waited, her head tilted back a little, her body straight. She didn't want to be intimidating, she wanted to be in control. And from the way Penelope dipped her head down, Ann knew she was. She breathed in softly, and let it out, while she waited.

"Yes, you see, well, Mary here was a daycare worker before, well, you know. So, we thought it might be good to take your suggestion. You know." She ended with a firm nod of her head before she looked at the other women for backup. The others nodded and smiled at Ann with hopeful little nods.

"That sounds excellent. I've got a notebook on the table over there. If you'd be so kind as to fill out a sheet with your basic information, who is in your group, what you'll be doing, things you might need, stuff like that, I'd appreciate it."

"Of course, Ann," Penelope said without any hint of huffiness.

Maybe she'd be alright, after all, Ann decided. This

leadership role wasn't something she'd ever planned to take. In high school, she and her friends had all encouraged each other, and had sometimes urged each other into a dare, but there hadn't exactly been a leader. She did her thing, they did theirs, and that's how it worked. Now, she'd been thrown in, feet first, and somehow, she'd learned to stand up.

She'd been worried she'd made an enemy out of Penelope, but it didn't seem she had. Maybe her mate had had a talk with her. Word probably got around about what happened. Ann wasn't sure who the woman was mated to, but whoever it was ranked lower than Rager, which meant he ranked below her too. Ann didn't really care, so long as the woman chilled out with her lady of the manor bullshit.

With a tired smile, Ann shuffled out the last of the women 15 minutes later. She went up to her room and sprawled on the bed. She'd been terrified, as always, but speaking at the podium like that had been the scariest thing she'd done in her life so far. Even the mating ceremony with Rager hadn't been that bad compared to public speaking. She'd managed it though, and everyone seemed content enough when they left. That was all that mattered really.

She wanted to build inroads with the wives, and she had plans. Plans like making sure Amanda had a role in the education of future children. Ann knew some of the revulsion over the wolves was simply that the humans didn't understand that they weren't in danger. They expected the wolves to turn into raving maniacal killers with huge teeth and claws at any minute. That wasn't how it happened.

After five years in the bunker with a wolf family, Ann knew first-hand what happened, and what needed to happen. It was all very silly, she thought, as she stuck her earbuds in and hit play. They didn't mind having the wolves in their homes during the day, but not at night? That was one of the reasons the wolves were housed away from the homes. People seemed to think dark-time meant murder-time to the wolves. It didn't.

She wanted to change those misconceptions, stamp out prejudice, and if that meant doing it one step at a time, that's what she'd do. She wanted Amanda and Stephan, and Rex even, to be able to do whatever they wanted to with their lives, and if that meant she had to stick her neck out for them, then so be it.

"Do you know that using candles to create heat is one of the simplest things you can do?" Skye asked Ann as they sat together over lunch the next day. Ann had invited her over before she left the day before, and now, they were outside in the garden.

"Candles? How?" Ann had learned quite a bit about the woman already, but the main thing she'd learned was that Skye was a survivor. She was bi-racial and had grown up with a lot of flack from people about it, and that had turned her mind inwards. Rather than let it eat at her, she'd taken her solitude and had started creating solutions where she saw problems.

She had a scientific mind and that had led her into a nursing program at Washington State University. She'd been found last week, in a basement, still clueless that the world had sprung back to life. She was also a lesbian, and Rager had made an exception for her. She would still need to carry a child, but she wouldn't be forced to mate with a male.

Speaking of Rager, he'd been very busy over the last couple of days, he'd come home late each night, and left very early. She assumed he was working on something important, maybe to do with that meeting she'd walked into by accident. Or those men of his that hated her so much.

"Ann? Are you there, Ann?" Skye laughed and snapped her fingers near Ann's face.

"What? Oh, I'm so sorry. I completely zoned out. So rude of me." Ann's face scrunched in apology. "Tell me about the candles."

"You need a lot of them and a lot of terracotta pots, but it works if you do it right. That was one way I kept warm. I also used a bike that I'd rigged up as a generator. It was connected to a battery, which I had connected to an inverter, and as long as I rode the bike often enough to keep the battery charged, I could run a small heater."

"Wow. No wonder you're so fit!" Skye was very svelte, and her body was covered in muscles with a lot of definition.

"I was bored, and I couldn't read textbooks all day, so

I worked out a lot too. Which also helped me to stay warm."

"Didn't you tell me you lined the basement with cardboard?" Ann prompted, curious as to how Skye had survived so long, alone and without a bunker to keep her warm.

"Yeah, that came from the bookstore too. I wore a lot of clothes, and was lucky to find some sub-zero gear too. I had a couple of sleeping bags that were made for that too. Some nights, I wasn't exactly sure I'd wake up the next morning, but I did. I got really tired of eating dried food and canned food, but I survived."

"You didn't do bad, at all," Ann complimented. "I really admire your ingenuity. I'm not sure I'd have survived without my Dad. We were in a bunker one of his clients gave him when he couldn't pay his legal fees. It was well-stocked and quite cozy, really. I'm not sure how long we'd have all lasted down there, but, well, it didn't turn out to be as bad as I thought it would be when we first went down."

"You'd have survived, you have that drive. I can see it in your eyes." Skye nodded her head wisely, her lips pursed in confirmation. "You would have found a way. It wasn't like one day it was warm, and the next the ice age showed up. We had time to prepare, and I could see what was coming when we got that first super-early snow. I started hauling food and supplies down to the basement."

"Did you find a gas stove or anything you could use?" Ann wondered aloud.

"I did and used it for heat when I cooked. I had to crack a window when I did, to make sure I didn't kill myself with gas fumes, but it kept the basement toasty. I ended up going through my supply before the aliens found me, but I had a small electric hotplate I'd connect to the bike setup when I couldn't stand the thought of cold beans again."

"That's really smart." Ann looked down at her hands, and wondered if she should ask the next question she had. She looked at the smile on Skye's face, and decided it was best not to bring it up. People's pasts were dangerous places to tread, mainly because most people had lost everyone that was special to them.

Ann was lucky, she had her parents, her neighbors, and Rex. Although Rex was a dick, he was still a part of her past. Most of the people she'd met hadn't been so lucky. And so far, the children she'd seen when they first left the bunker were the only ones she'd seen. She hadn't seen any since.

"I guess I just had a lot of time to think things through, down there on my own. It's funny, I'd noticed it had started to warm up in the basement, but I thought I was cracking up. When the aliens came down to bring me out, I thought I had died, and we'd got the afterlife all kinds of wrong." Skye scoffed at her own joke. "I really didn't know what to think when they gave me an address for an apartment and let me go. With the reminder that I'd have to have a child before I turned 38."

"What if you can't?" Ann had worried about that question too.

"Apparently they have ways of fixing problems." Skye grimaced uncertainly. "I don't know what that means."

"Maybe it means they have some kind of medical equipment on the ship that we can use down here. We're all expected to have babies, but they haven't told us a thing about how they expect us to give birth and not die." Ann's voice rose at the end, a sign of her fear.

"I'm sure they have stuff up there to help us. And I'm going to focus on studying obstetrics, Mary's going to start studying pediatrics, and Meg's going to focus on general medical care. It won't be perfect, but if they don't have tech and help up there that could make this easier for all of us, well, we'll just hunt down the supplies we need and take care of it ourselves. I promise."

Somehow, Ann didn't doubt that Skye would keep her word. "Thanks. I needed to hear that. I'm terrified about it, but I can't really talk to my mate about it, can I? I don't think he's afraid of anything in this world."

"They're scary, aren't they? Those aliens? Sexy as fuck, but scary." Skye smirked at Ann's shocked face. "Hey, I'm gay, not blind. Those are some fine men that came out of the sky, I can't lie about that. Doesn't mean I'd want to sleep with any of them, but I can admit they have great genes. Hopefully, we'll all have pretty babies out of this whole thing."

"I hope so." Ann settled back into the white folding chair she was in and looked around. Her cow was out in the field, asleep in the warm afternoon sunlight. "I still can't believe you didn't know. You must have been really surprised when you came above ground."

"Floored, really. I'd managed to get the basement at a constant temperature, but as I said, it had started to warm up. I thought I'd hit some point where maybe I didn't need to exercise because those cold walls finally warmed up a little, from the inside out. I was still trying to puzzle it out when they came for me." Skye laughed, her eyes on the wispy clouds overhead. "I thought I'd never see clouds again."

"We're still waiting on rain and we have no idea what the seasons will be like, but my guess is, the aliens will make sure we don't have anything too bad. They had the tech to end a new ice age, so I have to guess they can keep it at bay."

"I hope so. I do not want to live in a basement ever again. Even if I did clean the potty out once a week, and clean the place every day, it started to smell a little funky down there. And I don't think I could do it all on my own again. That shit was hard."

"I can only imagine. I think I'd have lost it."

"Maybe. Maybe I did, and this is all a hallucination? Who knows? It's as good as any other explanation I've heard so far." Skye sat back in her seat, her blue eyes dancing with mirth. "Maybe we're all crazy?"

The serious expression in her eyes made her smile seem frozen, maybe even broken, and for a moment Ann's heart hurt for the other young woman. "Maybe we are. I remember hearing about a theory that we were all players in some kind of cosmic video game, and that this wasn't real. That our reality wasn't real. And the more I thought about it, the more my brain just twisted up into a knot. All we know, for sure, is that our reality is real, don't we? My reality isn't yours and vice versa. And let's stop there before I get a headache."

Both women laughed with the humor of the moment, and the sad part passed. Ann was glad she hadn't asked Skye about her family now. It might have proven too painful if she had. For both of them.

"Can I ask you something?" Skye said softly, her voice barely even registering.

Ann bit her lip but nodded her head. She was a leader now, right? She couldn't show fear or back off from answers that people sought from her. "Sure."

"What's it like to be married to one of them? Mated, whatever they call it." She didn't look judgmental, she looked like she simply wanted to know the answer to something that puzzled her deeply.

"It's great for me. I mean, they're just like human men, physically, and my mate and I are one of the lucky ones that are truly, I guess soulmates is the word? We just click. And it's like any other marriage from before. It's intense though, the way we are with each other, and well, a lot more than I expected, really."

"Cool. So, it's not like they beat you and make you have sex with them?" She looked like that might have been what she was afraid of.

"Not at all. When you go through the mating ceremony, you're joined, so you feel sexual desire for each other, that's the point, I guess. To make babies. But, it's a bond, and a little piece of what makes you who you are, is joined to a little piece of him, it's really amazing to see, I can tell you that. But you become a part of one another, and abuse or rape would be out of the question. They wouldn't do that to themselves, so they don't do it to their mates, who are a part of them now."

"I'm really glad to hear that. I didn't want to be impolite, but it really bothered me, wondering if all of you were abused, and I was some lucky case that will probably be alone for the rest of her life without a mate."

"I hope you aren't alone. I really do. But, until your

lucky lady shows up, you're welcome here if you get lonely. Especially during the day. You can go on my little expeditions with me, if you'd like." Ann waited for Skye to finish squinting at her.

"Expeditions? What are those?"

"I'm hunting down supplies, everything we might need. The men are doing it, of course, but they're looking for immediate needs. Clothes, food, things like that. I'm looking for more seeds, medical equipment and supplies, books, all kinds of things."

"Sure, that sounds great. Meg and I are doing classes in the evenings, so my mornings are free. We could all join you, if it would help?"

"Yeah, sure that sounds great. The more the merrier. I do have one rule, though." Ann's face tensed, and she looked away before she turned back to Skye, her expression very serious. "No valuables are to come back to our area. None. Jewelry, guns, paintings, anything like that, none of it can come back to this place. I just, I don't want people fighting over glittery pieces of rock, or oil paint that's mixed in an awesome fashion, ever again. Does that make sense?"

"It does, yeah. I agree. When do you want me to be here?"

"Around 8 am would be good. We can get back before lunch then, unless we find a lot of stuff. Then I'll call a crew of soldiers to bring a truck to load it up. Oh, and I have to take guards with me, wherever I go."

"No problem. I can understand why. I've heard things, things I don't like. Things that sound far too familiar, for my taste."

"About the wolves or about Rager choosing me for a mate?" Ann decided to be blunt and open about both problems.

"Both of those, actually. I would hope this new world had space enough for all of us to live and get along in." She didn't look happy about the fact that it wasn't. "But no, there are some whiny bitches out there, thinking that some dirty… wolf is taking their man. Or there's a man out there that thinks you're a skank whore that shouldn't be married to the Supreme Overlord, or whatever he's called. It's all insanity." Her eyes rolled, but then she perked up. "At least you aren't as insane as the rest of them."

"Wait before making that decision!" Ann laughed and poured more tea into their glasses. "You might find I'm the worst of the bunch. I have a lot of ideas about what the world should be like, and which way we should head in the future. If I have my way, the Earth just isn't ready for the kind of peace I have in mind. Or maybe it is. She shook off most of the population like they were an infestation of fleas, didn't she?"

"You've got that right, Ann. I think the world is ready

for exactly that, and if that's the direction you want to go in, I am 100 percent behind you, girl. Lead us on." Skye lifted her glass and Ann tilted hers against it until they tinkled. Maybe the future she dreamed about was possible, after all.

11

A week passed, a week of late nights, late mornings, and sweet little gifts from Rager. He'd taken the day off, and they were out in his transporter so they could explore the city together.

"There are parts that even my soldiers haven't explored yet," he said as he put the transporter down on a clear spot between two very tall buildings and turned the machine off. "None of us have been out here, and I assume you haven't either?"

He turned to her with a smile and she shook her head. "No, I don't go this far out, even with that soldier you assigned to me."

"Good. It's not necessarily dangerous but the breeding group has started to let animals out and some of them might be aggressive." They stepped out of the transporter together and walked out into the debris of what had once been part of a major city. "Not that we've really started on predator animals yet."

"I wish you'd leave snakes off the list," she said as she walked beside him, her eyes on the buildings. She scanned each one to categorize them into things that might be useful. A pharmacy that had likely been ransacked already, a jewelry store that was also likely empty, and a few more. Clothes, food, survival. That's what she mainly wanted and she found those on the other side of the street.

"But they control rodent populations," he answered and waited for her to finish her roundup. "We've already seen some rats in other parts of the country. It won't take them long to breed enough to travel."

"Non-venomous snakes then, please. Let's look in the camping store first, shall we?" she asked and headed in that direction. She glanced back and saw he watched her with amusement. "What's so funny?"

"Nothing, just your dislike of things that slither. You aren't afraid of my tongue, thankfully."

"Or your fingers. But right now," she paused and turned to him with a flirtatiously impish look, "we need to see if there's any survival gear left in this little store. Focus, Rager."

She didn't exactly try to stop the way her hips

swayed as she walked into the open door of the bedraggled shop.

They didn't find much in the shop, a few cylinders of propane, some lantern wicks, but some rain jackets in bags and a few tents might prove useful to others in the future. Rager loaded those into the transporter and met her at the pharmacy. There she found some gauze, a few plastic toys, and some braces for a variety of joints that might be sprained. They put those in the transporter too. She looked down the aisle for women, and found a few things she could use. She crammed a few bottles of lotion into a backpack she carried and the packs of tampons and pads that she found.

She turned around to scan the shelves behind her and found boxes of pregnancy tests and not much more. She left the tests where they were, fear a knot in her throat. Others might be happy to use them, but she didn't want to take them. Not right now. This was all still new to her, and she didn't want to think about it. Not yet.

"Find anything in the men's section?" she called out and walked over to him. She found him in front of a display of razors.

"I can't believe you were all still using these," he said, mystified.

"Well, your little light zappers aren't permanent

either, I noticed," she said, a little miffed, but deep down she knew his remark hadn't really stung, she was simply reacting to the sight of the pregnancy tests still.

"No, I don't mean that, I meant that the technology is so old. We designed our system to allow hair to grow back, if it was wanted, but these were so brutal, and caused so many problems that we left them hundreds of years ago." He looked up at her and she quickly turned to look at the razors.

"We were working on laser hair removal. It was still new to us, though, and really expensive."

"You all placed value on the strangest things," he said and they left the store. "Shall we have lunch over there?"

She turned to look at where he had pointed. There used to be a tiny café between two of the shops, and a table and two benches, all made of concrete, were still there. "Sure, that looks like as good a place as any."

She unloaded the food from the transporter and Rager brought some tableware with him. Together they filled their plates with a bean casserole that she'd thought up and some salad. She had a couple of glass bottles filled with tea and they sipped at that as they ate.

"The cream is from our cow," she told him proudly. She'd searched quite a few books before she found the one that told her how to make sour cream and butter from cow's milk. She'd also learned about pasteurizing the milk to make it safe. She'd been glad when she found that section.

"Is it? It's very good," he said and added another dollop to his casserole. It was made from pinto beans and spiced with some of the lovely spices she'd found in her explorations. "I'm glad you're settling into this, Ann."

"It's not been easy. So much has changed. But then, I guess it has for you as well. What kind of food do you have on your planet?" It had only just occurred to her that there might be different plants and animals there.

"We mainly eat a vegetarian diet, as we do here, but we have more fish. Some you don't have here because they died out long ago, or they bred into different kinds, but most of the things are the same. We even have cheese on our planet."

"I've tried to make some cheese. I miss that stuff. We'll see in a few weeks how well I've done." She didn't say that she had a lot of hours to fill in the day since he'd started to work so much. She just told him about the things she'd done. "I'm glad you've taken today off. Kind of."

"It was time. We needed some time together. You've been looking… stressed." His eyes examined her, and she felt like a bug under a microscope. "What's wrong?"

"Nothing really. I'm just very busy. It leaves me tired, all the things I manage to get done in a day. When we were still in the bunker there wasn't a lot to do. Sometimes I'd stay awake for two days reading a book, then I'd sleep a few more. There wasn't a lot to do. Even when we tried to stay busy, there were times when I was actually bored."

"I would hate to be locked away like that for so long." He rested his elbows on the table and looked at her, his head propped in his hands. "I'm glad we came here."

"Were you considering going somewhere else then?" She smiled but she watched him, curious.

"There were a couple of planets we considered. Earth was the most like ours, though, we just needed to thaw it out."

"And repopulate it." She'd meant it as a joke, but in the back of her mind, she cringed. Why did she have to bring that up?

"That too. We'll try it this way, and if it doesn't work, well, we'll just gestate a few thousand people in the same lab where we're bringing animals back to life."

"That sounds like a cold way to go about it. They'd have no parents. What would it be like for them? How would you do it?" She waited for an answer, but he shook his head.

"It would have to be cloning, so they'd have had parents, but it would have been a long time ago. We'd find DNA where we could and reproduce it in the lab."

"That's how you're reproducing the animals?" She

thought about her lovely cow, and wondered if she'd lived before.

"Yes, but we have to be careful. We don't want to bring some of your people back, do we?" He laughed, but she could see he was serious.

"No, you're right. Some people are better left dead."

"Exactly. So, we'd rather reproduce humans the natural way. To give them all a chance at having a good life."

"Couldn't your lab tweak the genes though? Make sure that things like mental illness and physical disabilities didn't exist?"

"We could, yes. But what would that get us? A world that looks exactly the same, across the board. We don't look at those things as bad, Ann. We do work to make sure the people with these disadvantages are cared for, however. We try to help them lead positive lives, too."

"I like that." She propped her own head on her hands and looked at him. "What do you want to explore next?"

"Your body, my sweet, but we need to check that hotel and the other building before I can explore you."

"Hm. I think you should do me then the other." She made sure there was a twinkle in her eye as she looked at him. He leaned closer to her, as if he wanted to crawl over the table and kiss her. But he leaned back, took a deep breath, and shook his head.

"No, duty calls. Your people need things we can't give them, so we must hunt them down."

"Fine, but I won't be happy about it. What are we looking for specifically?"

"You can be as grumpy as you like, Ann." He stood up with a wink and smiled. "We're looking for bedding, beds, room dividers, things like that. I thought a hotel would be the best place to look."

"You're right. Won't we need another transporter?" she asked and followed behind him. When she caught up to him, she placed her hand in his. She smiled when his fingers closed around hers and he didn't let go.

"One will come tomorrow if we find what we need." He pulled her hand up to his mouth and kissed it. "Let's see what we find first."

They found a lot of dust on the first floor, but beneath that, they found the laundry with bedding nestled in plastic tubs. Everything they could want for a bed was there, and upstairs there were quite a few hundred single and double beds to take. Room dividers weren't really an option, but they did find those in the next building. They were dividers for workstations but they would do the job.

"Why do you need all of this?" Ann asked as they finally left the two buildings and boarded the transporter.

"We have a load of people coming in from Illinois.

We're going to put them in the hotels in our sector, but a lot of them will have to stay in other shelters. We don't have enough houses or apartments cleared for all of them yet."

"Ah, I see." She nodded as he guided the transporter off the ground. "That sounds like a huge amount of people."

"They were all in a bunker up there, some kind of government facility. I expect a few might be trouble, but we'll soon have them settled in. I hope. Otherwise, life won't be pleasant for them."

"What do you mean?" She was puzzled and looked at him. "I thought you weren't going to have a prison here?"

"That was the idea, but I should have known better. Some of your people are so… selfish, Ann. I've never encountered it before, not until I came here. It's staggering, really."

"It can be, especially if you haven't seen it before." Ann's thoughts were on Rex, but she didn't say it. "It's hard to get used to, and honestly, I don't think you ever do."

"No, and it seems we can't show them a better way, so we're putting the ones that break too many rules, or go too far in a place down toward Mexico. They're kept alone out there, where they can't hurt anyone here."

"Unless they join together," she pointed out, not sure

it was a good idea at all. "That's when you get problems, when like-minded people join up and hatch up plots." She trod carefully and chose her words as best she could. She didn't want him to even think about people like Rex.

It would kill Amanda and Stephan if Rex were discovered, and it might hurt her parents, too. And her, in the long-run. She already had enough people that hated her, she didn't need to add to it. For now, Rex hadn't hurt anyone, he'd just been himself and hot air. Maybe he'd calm down once wolves started to have more freedom.

"I have thought about that," Rager finally said, his voice an intrusion into her thoughts. "We keep it guarded, and they aren't allowed to go near each other and there's no way for them to communicate. Hopefully, that will keep them quiet until we can figure out what to do with them."

"I'm sure you'll think of something." Ann patted his shoulder and looked out as the landscape passed down below. So much had been destroyed, so much had changed, why did people still want to hang onto greed?

The world was at their feet, whether they were on their own or with the aliens. People weren't forbidden from scavenging; they could go out and get whatever they wanted. It was there for the taking, so why were greed and selfishness so prevalent in their society?

The world had almost ended for them all, yet pettiness still existed. People like Penelope still wanted to feel superior. People like those in the prison still wanted to take from others. It didn't make any sense, not when there was so much to take.

"People are stupid," she said, at last, and let her seat down to close her eyes. Exhaustion had suddenly hit her and she just wanted to close her eyes.

"Are you alright?" he asked, a note of concern in his voice.

"Fine, just a little tired. I'll be alright."

"Okay."

She heard a few buttons beep, and then she could hear the familiar strains of one of her favorite bands. They'd called themselves Elixyr, and they'd made New Age music. Sort of a blend between Celtic ballads, trance music, and Gregorian chants. It was odd, but Ann liked it because of that. It also soothed her when she wanted noise but nothing too dramatic.

His thoughtfulness made her smile, and she drifted into a place where she was aware of what happened, but she might have been dreaming too. There was a blank moment and then Rager stood over her, a smile in those startling orange eyes.

"We're home, my queen."

"Queen? Huh?" She struggled up and he moved away. "How did we get here so quick?"

"You fell asleep, and yes, queen. I'm the master of this world, I can make you my queen, can't I?" He laughed and moved away. "If you aren't too tired, I'd like to show you how I worship queens. Well, queen. You're the only one I need, after all."

Her heart melted and she took his hand. Maybe not all of the people in the world were stupid, after all.

12

"Thanks for the lift, Ann. It would have taken me ages to walk out here," Skye said and Ann guided the transporter through the sky.

"No problem. I need to visit my mother anyway. I haven't been over in a few days now." It had been a few days since she and Rager had gone on their excursion and she was restless at home. He would come home late and leave even earlier than he had before. She'd barely seen him since that day.

"I've heard something about this part of our sector," Skye started, then stopped. She looked as if she struggled with some inner argument before she carried on. "A lot of the problem wolves are out here."

Ann's blood went cold, and she looked at Skye with trepidation. Had she heard about Rex? Was Rex causing even more problems out here? Those stupid gang signs had shown up a lot more recently and Ann knew it was part of his even stupider resistance group behind it all. "Have you heard who's leading it?"

Ann had suspected this was why Rager was gone so much, that this resistance movement had started to gain traction and he was needed to stop it.

"No, but I've heard that some of the aliens..." she stopped and had that inner argument again before she continued. "Some of the aliens have joined with them, from what I've heard. They hate you, Ann. They think you're beneath them, and want Rager to cast you aside for an alien female."

"I've heard that once or twice now," Ann said softly and tried not to let her anger, or fear, come through. "It's been a problem since the day we mated."

"It's a huge problem if they've joined up with the wolves. They could make this a real battle."

"I'll talk to Rager about it when I get back. I'm sure he knows, but just in case, maybe it's time I made sure he's aware of it all."

"I'd be happier if you would," Skye sighed and relaxed in her chair. "You're the only person I like here, besides Meg. I can't lose you."

"I can't be the only one?" Ann asked, happy for the change of subject. Thoughts about revolutionaries and coups just made her angry and sad at the same time.

"Basically. Meg is great, but all she wants to talk

about is classes and training. You at least talk about other things."

"I'm not as deep as her, huh?" Ann teased, a hint of humor in her eye. When Skye looked upset, Ann relented. "I get it. Sometimes you just need to talk about something that isn't work."

"That's it. And we scavenge together, so that's cool too." Skye looked pleased and sat back. "Now, if only I could find a woman of my own."

"That's not what you're scavenging for, is it?" Ann teased and laughed. "Although, that might be the only place you find one now. Oh, there's a large group coming in tomorrow."

"Really? You mean it's possible?" Skye looked excited, and Ann was glad she'd told the woman. It wasn't a secret, but not everyone knew about it.

"I don't know, but the possibility is always there, isn't it? I mean, it's not like you're going to be attracted to a woman only because she's a lesbian, but the possibility is there that you'll find... someone." Ann didn't want her friend's hopes to get up too high, she'd hate to see her let down, but she did like to see her smile.

"Nah, you're right. But having new people might be nice. If they don't cause problems. Where are they from?"

"I have a feeling they're Chicago glitterati. Rager said

it was a government bunker, but I imagine there'll be more than a few of Chicago's finest in there."

"It's a shame, isn't it? All the people that are likely dead. Famous movie stars, music stars, all of them are probably dead, but some scummy politicians survive to feed off the public another day." Skye sounded more than a little bitter about it, but Ann couldn't blame her.

"It is a real shame, but Rager will make sure they know their place. That's one of the reasons my father is a mayor, he wasn't a politician before everything. He was just a man with some intelligence."

"Yeah, I figured they wouldn't want politicians in the new world they're building. I think they want people that will be able to lead, yes, but not people that will go on and on about 'this is America' until they get shot or whatever."

Ann laughed with Skye and set the transporter down in front of her mother's home. "You're right, they don't want that. Not because they want to stamp out America, or Americans, but because that kind of isolationism isn't what they want. They want people to see the globe as their home, not a speck of that globe. Then they might respect it a little more."

"I get you." Skye nodded as they left the transporter. "And I agree. We need to think like that, if we want to make this place better than it was before."

"Good. Want to meet me back here around 4, and we can go back?"

"Sure. I'll see you then. Thanks again!" Skye waved as she left, headed to the home of a woman that had found some ultrasound machines in the storage unit in her backyard. They wanted to make sure it all worked before they dragged it out to the clinic Meg had started to set up.

"I'm here, Mom!" Ann called as she walked into her mother's home. She found her mom, as usual, with Amanda in the kitchen.

"Hi, honey! We're making lunch if you're hungry?" Her mother came up, hugged her, and kissed her cheek before she walked back to the stove.

"What are you making today?" Ann could smell tomatoes and what smelled like cabbage.

"A kind of stuffed cabbage. We used some chickpeas as filling, and we're experimenting to see how it tastes."

"It sounds interesting, anyway." Ann sat down at the table and watched the two women work together. They'd always gotten along well, and after their time in the bunker, had become almost like really close sisters. Ann was glad they were able to stay together like this, she knew it would break both their hearts if they were separated, but Amanda deserved far more than to only be her mother's cook. "Amanda, have you got some of those lesson plans ready yet? I wanted to go over them with the ladies that are putting the curriculum together."

"I have, they're in a folder in the hallway for you." For a moment, Amanda's expression was sad, but it changed back to placid peace after a moment. "I hope it all goes well, and I'll be happy to help in any way that I can."

Ann knew Amanda meant 'allowed', and her heart broke. The woman was only dangerous a few nights out of the month, and as long as she locked herself up, she wasn't really a danger at all. How could anyone look at her and think she wasn't worthy of the same rights as anyone else? It made Ann angry, and more determined to make things change.

"Hopefully, you'll be able to do a lot more one day." It was all Ann could give her at this moment, but it was better than nothing. Hope was always better than defeat, wasn't it?

"Set the table, dear," her mother said from the stove, and Ann stood up to get some plates. It would just be the three of them. Stephan was with Ann's father, and they wouldn't come home for lunch.

Ann put down three plates, three forks, knives, and spoons, and three glasses. All three sets matched and the food would be the same; the only thing different would be the people that ate them. One could change shapes and became a wolf at certain times, while the other two remained human. Ann had become used to the whole thing over time, down in the bunker, and it didn't frighten her anymore.

She knew some of the wolves were bad, and had killed their own kind and plain people, but they were all gone, weren't they? Except for people like Rex. She glanced up and saw him through the window. He was mowing the lawn, his face angry and dissatisfied. He looked as if he was muttering as he pushed the old mower along, but then she saw the plastic in his ears.

She tried to wave at him, but he turned away, his middle finger high in the air. He'd seen her then. And dismissed her just as easily. Her heart clenched, a betrayal she hated.

He could still hurt her then, even now, when she was all but certain she loved her mate. She didn't want to be with Rex anymore, it wasn't that. It was the childhood they'd shared that he threw back at her now. It was the years in the bunker, and her efforts to make sure he and their families were safe that he so callously flipped off.

She'd always known he was selfish, as selfish as the men that Rager had sequestered away, but this was a new low, even for him. She'd known her love for him had started to wane, it had started to disappear the moment Rager first came to her in her dreams. But she'd still cared about him.

For him to be so nasty now wasn't just cruel, it was

callous. If he wasn't careful, his supervisor would see him and punish him, she thought. She watched as he came back to face her, his middle finger in front of a face filled with red-rage. She didn't back down, she didn't look away, she simply stood there, her head high as she stared out at him.

"What's the matter, honey?" her mother asked, and came up behind her.

"Oh, him." Her mother sighed, and pulled her away from the window. "Let him get on with his work, honey."

"I was, I wasn't doing anything to stop him," Ann protested, but sat down anyway.

"I know, but he's got a lot on his shoulders." Mary glanced towards Amanda, but didn't say anything else. She rolled her eyes and Ann had to stifle a laugh. When her mother mouthed the word 'men' and rolled her eyes again, Ann smiled and smothered another laugh.

"I guess you're right." Ann let it go because Amanda brought a bowl with her stuffed cabbages to the table and they all took a few of the rolls to try.

"It's not… bad." Mary chewed carefully around the hot food, her face scrunched up with uncertainty. "It's not what I was hoping for though."

"Too much rosemary, maybe?" Ann offered. She liked it, but there was an odd taste to it.

"No, I think it's dill. I had two similar bottles near

each other. One was basil, the other dill. I think I picked up the dill bottle." Amanda wrinkled her nose, but she kept eating. One thing people didn't do now was throw food away. It was too precious, even if it tasted weird.

"It's not bad, but it does explain why I keep getting a hint of pickle with each bite," Ann said, amused. "I thought I was going crazy."

"No, your mom's the one that'll be after pickles soon." Amanda looked guilty and then tried to cover it up. "She always did like her pickles in the summer. We barely managed to can anything some years because she'd eat most of it before we got anything in the jars."

"I did not. Okay, that one year I did, but those green tomato pickles were good."

"They were. Shame we didn't have many that year."

"We'll have plenty this year, as long as I can get the celery to grow," Mary said and stood up, her jeans a little tighter than normal, Ann noted.

Her mother had a secret, one she hadn't told Ann, but Ann knew she'd tell her soon enough. If her suspicions were correct. With a smile, Ann picked up her own empty plate and headed to the sink. "You two sit down, I'll wash up what's left and put the rolls away."

"Yes, put them in the freezer please, dear. We'll make something else for dinner." Mary sat down at the table and wiped at her face with a towel. Sweat had beaded at her forehead, something that concerned Ann.

"Why are you so hot, Mom? Want me to turn the thermostat down?"

"It's just a little nausea, Ann. It'll pass. Maybe I don't like pickles as much as I used to?" She tried to make a joke of it, but Ann wasn't buying it.

She'd let her keep her secret for now, Ann decided, and stuck her hands in hot, soapy water. She'd have to come over more often, she thought, just to keep an eye on her mother. And maybe she'd bring Meg and Skye next time. Both might be of service.

If her suspicions were correct.

The rest of the afternoon was spent in the garden, pulling weeds and trying to avoid Rex, but Ann saw him once more before she left. She knew it was a stupid thing to do, but they were on their own near the porch, and she really wanted to make him stop looking at her like that. She walked right up to him, determined to speak her mind. "Rex, I think it's time you listened..."

But she didn't get to finish, he just walked off, as if he hadn't heard her, or seen her. Like she was some kind of ghost that the world, the living world, couldn't see. He'd just treated her like she was nothing, and he was the one that the aliens considered beneath even her. Him and all his revolutionary buddies.

She wouldn't turn him in, she wasn't that kind of person, but she was done protecting him. If he could treat her like that, who knew how he'd treat her if he ever got the upper hand? That thought sent a cold shiver of dread down her spine. She didn't want to think about a day when that might happen. It was too horrible to consider.

ever got the upper hand? That thought sent a cold shiver of dread down her spine. She didn't want to think about a day when that might happen. It was too horrible to consider.

13

ann woke up and waited for a moment. She was alone, as usual lately, but it wasn't Rager she waited for. It was the telltale sign of cramps that she waited to feel. Her periods had always come at night, never during the day, and she would always wake up with cramps low in her abdomen. Not this morning. Or the last few either, no matter how much she waited for it.

She got up, went to the bathroom, but still, there were no signs that menstruation had started. She wanted to scream but knew that would just be silly. She took a shower, dried off, and got dressed in a pair of jeans and a green t-shirt. She'd have to go out and do what she hadn't wanted to do. Find a pregnancy test.

She drove to the apartment where Skye lived and asked her to come out exploring with her. Ann watched as Skye looked at her, noted the moment that Skye saw her anxiety, and took a deep breath. "I need to find something important."

"Sure, I'll come with you. I've got your back." Skye shut the door, and they left. Before long, they were at the pharmacy and Ann stared at the rows of boxes in front of her.

"Will they even be useful at this point?" Ann said it out loud so that Skye could hear her. She'd brought the other woman along simply as moral support. She was late, a lot late. That kind of late that got your attention, and she'd worried about it for far too long. It was time for some answers.

It had only just occurred to her that the tests might expire. She'd seen a date on one of the boxes and wondered if it was just a marketing gimmick to make women buy another one. It was just a strip with something on it, after all, wouldn't it stay good forever?

"Sometimes the more expensive digital ones will still work longer, but usually they all expire around two to three years after they were manufactured. Which means even the newest ones will probably be expired." Skye's voice came from a different part of the store. She walked over and looked at the boxes on the shelves. "Those might, and I can't stress that might enough, might work."

She pointed at the very expensive digital pregnancy tests; her face doubtful.

"Is there another way to tell?" Ann's voice shook as she reached for the box, her lip caught between her teeth as she read. She was a bundle of mixed-up emotions, strung too tight and ready to burst into tears or a fit of anger, she wasn't sure which.

"If we had the equipment, we could do a blood test. Meg and I have been looking for the equipment in hospitals. She's found one hospital with a lab that's intact. She might have it all up and running now, if you want to go and see her?"

"I think that might be best. But I'll take a few of these just in case." Ann grabbed a few boxes of the digital tests and stuffed them in her bag. "Let's go find her."

"She should be there now. I know a few of the women want confirmation, although it's more than obvious that there are two or three that are pregnant already. She's been working late to try to get it operational."

"I hope it's all working then. I have a feeling I know the answer, otherwise I wouldn't be here now. It's just that I would have liked more time with him, to get to know him better, but I guess progress waits for nobody, right?" Ann made sure Skye was settled into her seat and started the transporter.

"Nope, and we all know how babies are made, don't

we?" Skye laughed, but it wasn't mean, it was just an amused sound. "Not that I'll have that problem."

"Not for a while, at least," Ann reminded her, then thought it might sound spiteful. "I didn't mean it to sound like that. How do you feel about having a baby?"

"I'd love to have kids. I'm gay, not anti-kid or anything. I'm still a woman, you know?" Skye's laugh was patient this time. "I know some women, straight and gay, that never wanted kids, and that was their choice. Probably the best one considering what happened."

"I try not to think about things like that too much. It's a depressing pit of gloom." Ann glanced at Skye and saw her nod her head in agreement. "I think you'll have beautiful children. Especially if they look like you."

"Maybe so. I'd like to get the nursing school up and running though, and the medical clinic too. Then I'll pay the aliens back for bringing me above ground again."

"How long would you have stayed down there?" Ann asked, just to change the subject.

"Another month or so. I was rationing food, but would have run out eventually. Then I'd have discovered the new world above. And the aliens."

"Shocking, aren't they?" Ann smiled at Skye, but soon glanced back at the world around her. "Maybe after I talk to Meg, I'll find out more about the medical technology they brought with them."

"That sounds like a plan to me."

They both went quiet as Ann drove, but Ann's mind wasn't quiet at all. She kept swerving between anxiety about the whole process of being pregnant and producing a child with a man she barely knew, to feelings she'd never quite explored before. The idea of a baby, her baby, pleased her, made her smile in a way she never had before.

She felt things she didn't understand when she thought about a baby of her own. Maybe it was what made other mothers so happy, that love they talked about. She wasn't sure. She did know her breasts were sore, which was sometimes a sign of her period, and she'd been tired the last couple of days.

Not enough to say she was pregnant, but the missing period was. She turned her attention back to her driving and tried not to stress about it too much. She'd have to deal with whatever result she got, she knew that and for now, there was nothing she could do about it.

"Don't panic, Ann. We'll get you through this. And hey, we'll get some practice in before it's your turn if you are pregnant." Skye's smile was bright and a little more confident. "Those other ladies should have their babies before you do, so we'll be experts at it by the time we get to you."

"Oh, that's funny." Ann did laugh, despite her contradictory tone. "At least I won't be your first."

"Always a good thing, when it comes to medical stuff." Skye sat back in her seat and sighed. "I remember the first time I had to draw blood for my clinicals. There was blood every-fucking-where. I'm just glad it was another student and not a patient. I'd have died of shame."

"That bad, was it?" Ann relaxed a little and smiled. "I can just imagine how scared you were. I'd have been terrified."

"I was. I didn't want to do it, but it was part of our training for that class. I had to do it. I knew I should have waited to take that class, but oh no, I had to go and get it out of the way." Skye shook her head ruefully, and Ann smiled brighter.

"You're like me, you like to face your problems head on. But I bet, like me, you had to think about it for a little while before you did it."

"That's exactly how I am. I'll make a quick decision if I have to, but I'd rather have time to think about it. Then, I normally face the problem and get it out of the way. It's better than worrying about it for the rest of my life, right?"

"Right. Which is why we're headed out to see Meg. I have to know, even if it is still early. I can't keep worrying like this, it's stopping me from getting anything done."

"I understand. It's that hospital there, the one down

to the left there." There were two hospitals close together and Skye pointed out the correct one to Ann.

Ann guided the transporter down onto the rubble-strewn road between the two hospitals and turned it off. She looked at the building, once sparkling white with a red cross, but now faded to gray and pink. In the past, it had bustled with life as staff worked to save lives, but now, it was silent.

Ann had tried to ignore it since she left the bunker, but she had to admit now that most of the world was eerie. It was far too quiet without that hum of life from thousands, millions of machines, footsteps, and human voices. Sometimes, she thought she might still be in a nightmare of some kind, trapped in a coma that she couldn't get out of. But she knew this was reality now, even if it unnerved her at times.

"I'll show you where the lab is." Skye took the lead and walked through the open doors of the hospital. What had once been the emergency entrance was now desolate and oddly lacked furniture. Had someone taken the chairs and tables that normally waited here with all the people that used them?

Despite the passage of time and lack of buffing machines, the floors still squeaked under Ann's hiking boots and the brown loafers that Skye had on. She did note that the usual chill found in hospitals was gone, and that a new sound took the place of the hum of machines the hospital used to care for their patients. Ann listened but couldn't make out what the noise was.

"What is that sound?" she finally asked as Skye led the way.

"Pigeons. We think they flew here from somewhere in the south. Well, somewhere warm, anyway. They just showed up one day. I'm not sure there was anywhere warm left, before the aliens came, but there must have been. They've got nests in one of the exam rooms, the window was broken so they must have got in through there."

Ann could only shake her head and walk on. The idea that somewhere might have been warm still, unfrozen, hadn't crossed her mind, but it was possible. There might have even been people there that waited it out. Rager hadn't said anything, but she hadn't really seen him in the last three days.

Which was another issue with this maybe-baby. Would he be at work all the time? Would she be left on her own, the token wife, with the token baby? She'd heard the reports about some of the alien men that didn't want her to be with Rager, how they detested the idea of her having his child. How would they react to the news if she was pregnant with his child?

It was all too much to think about, and for the moment she decided, she'd focus on one thing. Was she pregnant or not? That was the main problem to focus on at the moment. The rest was irrelevant. She lifted her chin a little as she followed behind Skye, determined to see this through.

"Hi there!" Meg called out as they walked through a door ten minutes later. It was deep within the hospital on a lower level that they'd accessed through stairs. Nobody trusted elevators that had been hanging in place for five years through an ice age. Power or not, the elevators were scary without the proper inspections.

"Hi, Meg. I've brought Ann along to be our first patient if you've got the lab working?" Skye walked in and stood beside Meg. Meg had on a lab coat and her hair was pulled back in a no-nonsense ponytail.

"It just so happens that it is. I've just got everything running, and it's all in order. What can we do for you, Ann?" She turned to Ann, curiosity in her eyes.

"I, uh, I need a pregnancy test. One that works." Ann showed her the bag she'd filled with pregnancy tests and shrugged. "Skye said these weren't reliable anymore."

"Skye was right, honey. Come over here and sit down. Sorry about the arm of the chair." It was one of those chairs that you'd find in a phlebotomist's lab, with a section that stuck out to support the patient's arm while blood was drawn. "The weather wasn't kind to this poor thing and the covering disintegrated. I've wrapped a blanket around it, so it won't be so hard or scratchy."

"It's fine," Ann said offhand, distracted by her thoughts. Needle, blood, results. "How long will it take to get the results?"

She looked up at Meg, the kindness in the other woman's eyes almost brought tears to her eyes for some reason. Ann tried to blink them away, but it only made the moisture drop from her eyes. "Sorry, I seem to be weepy today."

"It's fine, Ann. Everybody reacts differently to this kind of test. I'll have your blood out before you know it, and the results should be ready in an hour or so."

"Alright. Good. So, I'll know today then?" She looked up to see Meg washing her hands before she doused them in something that looked like vodka. Meg brought the bottle over and dabbed some of the liquid onto some gauze. She swiped the inside of Ann's arm, placed the tourniquet, and started to look for a vein.

"Yes, you'll know today. And yes, that's vodka. I haven't found a bottle of alcohol in the supply rooms yet. Most of them have alcohol swabs, but those are all dried up. You might feel a pinch."

Ann hadn't noticed Meg had opened a kit, but when she looked down, she saw the needle in her arm, blood a rush of red through a clear tube that ran into a vial. Her head swam for a moment and she looked away. She'd never been good with blood, but she didn't want these two to know that. She was the de facto queen of the area, after all. "You will keep this quiet, won't you?"

"Ann, we're both aware of the danger you're in," Meg said without looking up, her concentration on the vial that now filled with blood. After a few more seconds, she took the vial away. The IV was removed and fresh gauze placed over the wound the needle left. "Neither of us will tell whatever we find out today. I promise you that. The aliens might make the law now, but we still respect our patients and the laws that used to govern us about them. They were there for a reason."

"Thank you, Meg. I appreciate all of this. I really do. You don't know how much I appreciate it." Now, to wait for the results.

"I'm sorry, I must have missed a step somewhere. From your own calculations, we should have something more conclusive than this. Let me work on it for a few more days and see if I've missed something." Meg looked crushed and Ann didn't want to make her feel worse about the failure of the test.

"So, do you think I am?" Ann had to ask, despite what Meg said.

"From what you've said, I think it's likely. I wouldn't swear on it though, Ann. Not without proof." Meg bent back down to the computer she was on and began to type into it again. "I just don't know what I could have gotten wrong."

"Thanks, Meg. I'll come back in a few days then." She picked up her bag and glanced over at Skye. "Do you want to come back to the house with me?"

Ann really wanted her friend to join her. She was crushed by the news that the test hadn't worked. She'd wanted the answer so badly!

"Yes, I'd like that. Come on, let's get you home."

"Thanks. See you, Meg," she called out as they left the lab.

"Bye, ladies. Have a good day."

"She'll be lost on that thing until she finds an answer," Skye said and they loped out of the hospital together.

By the time Ann set the transporter down in her driveway, she was boiling with curiosity. Skye followed along behind her, silent until Ann closed the door to the bathroom just off the bedroom. "I'll wait here, shall I?"

"Sorry, yes please." Ann dropped the bag down and opened it. She saved two for the morning and opened the other five. She found a collection cup in each box and sat down to get what she needed. When the cup was filled, she cleaned up, and followed the instructions for the digital tests. One didn't come on at all, the others all lit up.

"Ann, I have to tell you, those can give you false negatives or false positives now. They're out of date," Skye called through the door and Ann grimaced.

"I know, but I have to try."

"Stubborn ass," Skye muttered with a laugh. "Just like me. Has to know."

"Want to come in and wait with me?" Ann opened the door and the other woman walked in. Ann sat down on the toilet and Skye on the rim of the bathtub.

"How long have you got left?" Skye asked.

"A few more minutes. Not long." She sighed and crossed her arms over her breasts but that only made her wince, so she put her arms back down. They hurt so much and felt like two rocks on her chest. But, again, it was a common sign of her period.

"The pregnancy books have all kinds of symptoms listed when you're first pregnant, but those can be hard to go by. Especially if your body is just fucking with you."

"Right? I think I might be, but it's hard to tell. Half of it might be stress, we've been through a lot in the last few months, and that might be causing all of my symptoms. Who knows?" Ann knew she was babbling but didn't care. She just wanted the time to pass.

"Will they beep or something?" Skye glanced at the tests on the counter where Ann placed them.

"I think so. I didn't read the rest, just the instructions on how to do the test part." Ann picked up the box and looked at it. She felt like she'd been waiting for results for hours now, and it only made it worse to know that these tests would probably give her false results. But she had to see what happened. "Yeah, they'll beep."

At last, she heard five beeps, one after the other. Skye

took her hand and they looked down at the tests. All five were positive. "What does that mean?"

"Unfortunately, nothing. They could be right, or they could be wrong." Skye sighed and hugged her close. "I'm sorry but that's the truth of it. You're no closer to knowing than when you started this morning."

"I hate not knowing!" Ann's frustrated tears fell, and she pulled away from Skye to wipe them away.

"And I hate it for you." Skye opened the door and walked out to the bedroom. "I'm going to get you something to drink and maybe something to eat. What do you want?"

"Just a sandwich or something," she replied miserably. "I'm sorry I'm not very good company today."

"It's fine, girl, don't worry." Skye made the call and went out to sit on the balcony. Ann followed her and sat down with her. "Look, I'll bring you some of those pregnancy books I found in the clinic, just in case, and you can prepare yourself, just in case."

"Thanks, that would be good. I don't know a lot about it, only what I had to learn in school and from other women I know." Ann thought about her mom, and decided asking her about pregnancy right now wasn't a good idea. Mary had her own troubles to deal with having Rex in her household. "I'm glad you're here with me."

"I'm glad too. It's nice having someone to talk to."

Skye settled back into her chair and looked out, but Ann knew she wasn't really seeing the landscape. She had something on her mind. "Are you sure you want those tests lying around like that?"

"Oh! You're right. What can I do with them though? If I leave them in a bag here a servant might find them, or Rager."

"I'll take them with me and dispose of them for you. Keep the two you've saved, and I'll take the rest."

"Thanks, Skye. You saved me some trouble."

"No problem. I just don't want you getting in a predicament if you don't have to. I know up here, in your compound, you're safe, but I hear things out there." Skye waved at the ether, at the life outside of the walls that surrounded the house. "The men are getting more pissed off, and the women are too. Everyone is, it seems. It's so bad, I rarely go out in the evenings now."

The new people that Rager brought in weren't settling in well. Two had already been taken off to the prison he'd alluded to, or so Skye had heard, and four were on the verge of it. All of them had been the leaders of the group, and had felt they should have some say in what happened in this new world because of it. Two had been senators before the cataclysm and seemed to think the US government still existed. Rager had swiftly shown them it didn't, and that he wouldn't bow to their demands.

"What will make those people happy?" Ann wondered aloud without realizing it. She looked at Skye in surprise when she replied to the question.

"Nothing. Being sent back to Illinois? I don't know, but a lot of them are joining forces with the wolves. They didn't have any wolves in their group, but they see them as allies. Unlike some of the people that are just terrified of them."

"That's good in a way, I suppose." Ann let her head fall back on the chair and felt the stiff soreness in her neck. "I don't know why people waste so much energy on giving up their lives. What does it matter now if you're from Illinois or Montana? We're all human and right now, we don't have the luxury of wasting all of this time arguing. It's a shame, really."

"You're right, Ann," Skye agreed and turned to face Ann. "I don't understand it either. I was training to put people back together from accidents, not wars. I couldn't stand working on someone knowing they'd tried to kill another human being and had ended up with me instead. It's senseless, really."

"Rager doesn't want war, either. His people aren't warmongers. He wants this place to be peaceful, like his own planet." She looked at Skye, sadness in her eyes. "I don't think our people will allow it. Wolf or not."

"It's that ingrained in us, isn't it?" Skye looked away

and winced with annoyance. "The same old story, time after time."

"In a way, it is, yes. No matter what kind of ideology we follow, what kind of government we put in place, people in power always lead us to war." Ann was disgusted, but at least it distracted her for a moment. "Why can't we just see that we can't continue like that? There aren't enough of us anymore."

"I don't think the aliens will allow our numbers to increase like that again," Skye mused, speculating now. "I think, once we reach a certain number, they'll start to control the population."

"What makes you think that? I don't disagree, but why do you think that?" Ann went to answer the door and brought in a tray with two sandwiches, some sliced vegetables, and two glasses of apple juice.

"I think that because they won't want to spread themselves too thin. That, and we were not going to be able to sustain the status quo for much longer, not the way things were going. That outbreak of super-measles in December 2019 nearly got out of hand. And that virus that was blinding people in Canada had started to spread down to us too. Then there was the rest of it. It was all just… getting out of hand. I don't think we had long."

"So why do we keep repeating it?" Ann asked, her

hand on her stomach. "Why do we women put up with it?"

"That's the million-dollar question right now, isn't it?" Skye looked at Ann with a look that almost made Ann shiver. "I'm not certain we should put up with it."

"We have power now, power that the men want, that the men need," Ann said it softly, a spirit of revolution growing in her own heart, but it was a spirit that marched in time with Rager's. With him, not against him.

"I think we might have something here, Skye." She leaned back, sipped her drink, and took a nibble from her sandwich. After she swallowed, she smiled and looked at her friend. "It's us that have been left to organize things and create what we need. Perhaps we should work on what we really need. To stop this nonsense about revolution and focus on making lives the best we can for all of us, not just a few."

"How do we do that, though? We've tried so many times in the past. We've overcome a lot, but men still think they have to march off to fight a king's war and we have to cater to them for it. They die for what? To be free of one yoke only to put on another? At least Earth men do. How do we stop that?"

"I'm not sure we can, but the aliens can. I know this much." The flare of spirit quivered a little, but didn't quite die down. "They won't put up with much, and they have the power to turn this place into an ice sheet again if they want to. I don't want to see that happen."

"You have some influence with Rager, don't you?" Skye asked, and took a bite of her sandwich. "You need to start talking to him."

"I try not to say too much about what's happening here. When he comes home, he's had a hard day…"

"Fuck that, and fuck him. He's the ruler here, he needs to hear what you're concerned about. You need to stop being the little woman, and start being the leader you're meant to be." Skye's bright blue eyes burned with icy fire as she spoke and Ann listened.

"But I'm not a leader. Not a very good one anyway. I had to insult Penelope just to get the luncheons to turn into something meaningful."

"You did, but you did it because you knew you had to. And you haven't backed down. I want you to rise a little higher, honey, keep moving up. And talk to your mate, for fuck's sake. Help us."

"Of course," Ann answered automatically, but she blinked. How could she interrupt his quiet time?

"Ann, look. I know you want to care for your husband, but if you die, if that baby you think you're pregnant with dies because you didn't speak up, I'll kill myself and haunt you!" Skye huffed and glared at Ann, but then she softened it all with a smile. "You have to think of more than just taking care of Rager now. You have to think of that baby, the rest of us, your people, Ann. Guide us and lead us, even if that means following an alien leader. Bring us this life you dream of."

It was all very surreal to Ann, but she heard Skye, and understood her. She'd been playing at being a leader with the women at her luncheons, but she'd not truly been a good leader yet. Not until she did all she could to make sure people were safe, happy, and healthy. And that meant talking to Rager about a lot.

She hadn't wanted to inconvenience him, but now she could see that was stupid. She'd been keeping things from him that he probably needed to know. "I'll talk to him tonight. If I can manage to stay awake. I've been falling asleep really early. I get so tired suddenly, and then I'm gone."

"That's probably another symptom," Skye said in an offhand way as she bit into her sandwich again. "Try, and if nothing else, write him a note and leave it for him."

"I hear you," Ann said, and took another bite. She chewed and thought about everything Skye had told her. She'd start with her Mom, she decided. She'd go see her tomorrow and talk to her about this baby stuff, and the rest of it too.

"I bet my Mom already has a plan in place. Her and Amanda, they're both always whispering to each other.

Two peas in a pod, those two." Ann laughed and finished her sandwich.

"I'm glad you still have your mom." It was a subtle reminder, but one Ann still heard. Most people in the world no longer had a mother. Even the group from Illinois was mainly single people or couples, no children or parents had made it into the bunker there.

"I'll want to speak to the women from the bunker too. Let's arrange something for them. Rager said they were being put into what basically amounts to crisis shelters. I can't blame them for being angry about that. Maybe we can sort out better accommodations for them."

"That would be a start, I believe." Skye winked at Ann before she spoke again. "Good start."

Ann smiled, not sure she was ready for all the things she now had on her plate.

15

"Mom! I'm here!" Ann called out the next day as she walked into her mother's home.

"We're in here, dear," Amanda called back from the living room, and Ann followed her voice. "Oh, I'm sorry, I didn't mean to interrupt."

"No, it's fine, come in, meet the other ladies." Mary started to introduce women that were either married in the old-fashioned way to other mayors or were mates of lower-ranking soldiers in Rager's force.

Ann smiled politely and greeted each one as she was supposed to, with a nod and a slight dip of her head. It was the way she'd learned to greet the women that came to her own luncheons. She hadn't known her mother still had the same thing with the lower-ranked officials of their sector.

There wasn't really a hierarchy set in place to follow, and now that she thought about it, she understood that it had been the ladies themselves that had created it. She'd soon put a stop to that. There'd be meetings of all the women soon, she thought, and decided that part of the empty hospital would serve her purposes.

She wondered now how Skye had ended up at the meetings and figured it must have been something Rager had suggested. She made a note to ask her later and went about the business of being sociable. An hour later, the women started to gather together and say goodbye. Each one was pleased to speak to Ann, and they all walked away with little smiles on their faces.

Ann knew Rager had to maintain his image as the leader of the new world they were creating, and that hierarchy would naturally evolve, but this ass-kissing didn't suit her. She hated to see so many intelligent women turned into simpering simpletons. It just wouldn't do.

"Let me help you, Amanda," she said as Amanda began to clear dishes away. Ann noted that several women stopped to stare at her as she picked up dishes to take to the kitchen to be washed. Fuck them, she decided. She would lead by example, and if they didn't like it, they'd either get in line and learn or they'd fall out of that line. It was their choice.

"Thank you, honey, but you know you don't have to

help." Amanda quickly glanced behind them at the women that now whispered behind their hands. "You don't want to cause yourself problems."

"As I was recently reminded, I'm basically the queen of our world now, Amanda, and I can damn well do as I please." Ann winked at her old friend and walked ahead of Amanda to put the plates down. She walked back to the living room and picked up glasses and more plates to carry back. When she came back to the living room from dropping those off, she saw a couple of the women had picked up a few dishes too and now carried them back to the kitchen. Good.

Ann smiled and by the time all the dishes were gone the women had said their final goodbyes and left. Ann was up to her elbows in soap bubbles and dishwater when her mother finally came in to sit down. "Thank you, honey. I appreciate that."

"You're welcome, Mom. How are you?" Ann had noted Mary looked a bit pale and seemed tired today. More than normal, and she remembered her suspicion. She looked intently at her mother and saw her mother blush before she grinned.

"I have some news, baby. News that might seem dreadful to you, but, well, you're a big girl."

"What? What is it, Mom? Are you ill?" The idea had finally occurred to her, her mom might not be pregnant but sick! Ann rushed over, her hands wrapped in a towel as she sat down by her mother. "What's wrong?"

"Nothing's wrong, Ann." Mary laughed and brushed hair back from Ann's cheek. "I'm pregnant, honey."

"Oh." Ann had suspected, but to hear her mother confirm it was another matter. "I'm going to be a big sister?"

"Yes, you are."

"Oh." Ann was stunned, even if she had suspected. "That's so lovely, Mom. Are you okay?"

"I seem to be. I've waited to make sure, but well, it's been a few months now. I think it was when we were in the bunker. Oh, listen to me, I'm babbling. Anyway, I'm fairly certain now. I've waited long enough, and well, I've got this." Mary stretched the loose summer dress she wore over her stomach and Ann saw the bump that had started to form there.

"Mom!" Ann's hands came out and she wrapped them over the slight bulge. "It's so little."

"I never did get very big with you, this is a lot bigger already than I was with you, so it doesn't seem little to me." Mary laughed and touched Ann's cheek. "You're happy about it?"

"I am, Mom, as long as you're healthy and the baby is healthy."

"I'm an older woman, there are risks, but I should be okay. Amanda and I are keeping track of everything now." Mary looked at her friend and Ann could see the bond they had. It was a special one, and Ann was glad her mom had Amanda.

"And Dad? What does Dad think?" Ann could just imagine him, he'd either be quiet and ponder it studiously, or he'd be ecstatic.

"He's worried about me, my age and everything, but he's happy too. We always wanted you to have a sibling, but it was hard in the old world. So much time away from home with work, just to keep a house and the bills paid. Now? We don't have to worry about that, do we?"

"No, I suppose you don't. I'm happy for you, Mom." Ann leaned over and kissed her mom. When she turned around, she saw Amanda with a note in her hand. Amanda put it away, but Ann saw the symbol on it, the symbol she'd seen on the buildings, a wolf in a circle. Ann watched her, but turned back to the dishes, to see what she'd do. Out of the corner of her eye, she saw Amanda back up to the fire and drop something in before she quickly moved away.

"And what about you, Amanda, have you got news for us too?" Ann heard the way Amanda inhaled quickly before she sat down with Ann's mom.

"No, nothing to report for me. I never was very good at doing what I was told to do." Amanda played it all off, and laughed. "I can take orders here, but it doesn't mean I'm great at following them."

"I hope you're careful about that," Ann hinted, her eyes on the glass she now washed. "There are rumors going around, and I've heard there's trouble brewing."

She'd come out and been a little more direct about it, just in case.

"Yes, I've heard some of the soldiers aren't happy about you," Mary said and got up to dry the dishes Ann rinsed off. "We're both concerned about that, and we hope they're just rumors."

"So far, but a few men have gone too far in public. Rager has dealt with them." She missed him now and wanted to be in his arms, but she knew he had a lot to deal with. "Besides, I'm hidden away in that compound. Between that and the aliens that stand guard everywhere I go, I think I'm alright."

There was one outside now. They were on rotation, and Ann had learned to tell them to wait for her outside of where she was if she wanted privacy. Today, her guard stood watch outside her mother's front door.

"Good, I'm glad he's taking it seriously," Mary said, pecked a kiss on Ann's cheek again, and put the glasses away in a cupboard. "Now, what would you like to call your little brother or sister?"

Ann thought about it for a little while, plates and glasses were cleaned and then she spoke up. "Sarah if it's a girl, or Alistair if it's a boy."

"Okay, I can see Sarah, honey, but Alistair? Where on earth did you get that?" Mary looked at Ann astounded.

"I read it in a book once. I like the sound of it. We could call him Ally for short. I like it." Ann feigned hurt over the rejection of the name, but smiled. "It's not for everyone, I suppose."

"No, maybe not." Mary patted her arm and took the plates away. "Maybe Marcus, or Amos. I like those."

"Amos, Mom? You can't do that to a kid." Ann laughed and placed forks and knives in the sink to rinse. "That's a terrible name."

"It's a little old-fashioned, but I can't name him Ann, or Hans. That would be worse. Amos is at least an A-name. I'd like to name him with you in mind." Mary looked sentimental as she walked back to the sink. "My first baby needs to be part of my next baby."

"Then what about the girl's name?" Ann was confused, but that seemed to be her perpetual state lately, so much so she was almost used to it now.

"I'll name her Sarah for you and give her your name as a middle name."

"Mom! That's so sweet!" She was the one to lean over to kiss a cheek this time. "Thank you."

"Well, I don't want you to feel left out or unloved. It will be odd enough for you having a baby brother or sister as an adult."

Ann didn't add that she might have a baby of her

own on the way. She'd come to ask for her mother's guidance on the matter, and a few other things, but her mom's news had changed her direction. She'd let her mom have this day, and talk to her about her own concerns later.

"I just want you both to be healthy, that's all I care about. Oh, go see Meg at the hospital. She's got a clinic and she's reviving stuff at the hospital. She might even be able to take an ultrasound of the baby." Which sparked her own idea. Maybe Meg would be able to do one on her? "Do you know how far you have to be to see the baby?"

"Around 6 weeks, I think. I was two months along when I saw you on a scan for the first time. They had to do the one that they put up in you though. I hate those, so disgusting." Mary shivered, and then saw Ann's face. "Right, you weren't old enough for those when we went underground, and then you've not had any tests or anything. How do I explain this, Amanda?"

"It's like a wand, they put it up, ahem, inside you, and have a look around from below." Amanda's cheeks were as red as her mom's and Ann laughed a little at them.

"I don't think I like the sound of it either. It sounds invasive!"

"It is, but it does the job."

"I'm almost glad I've missed all of that," Ann said and let the soapy water drain from the sink. She doubted she was far enough along to have a normal ultrasound if you had to be that far along to see the baby. That wouldn't tell her anything then. Unless Meg had that device her mom mentioned. As far as she knew, it was the normal version of an ultrasound. She'd had one done on her stomach once when she was a child and had a very bad infection, so she was familiar with them.

"I would say you should be, but those exams are good to have, or were. They caught a lot of cancer and other problems women have," Mary said softly, and looked at Amanda. "It's not all roses, without our technology."

"No, it's not, but we're working on it," Ann told them, and leaned back against the sink, the dishes done. "We're trying to find out what women need, in one of my groups. What kind of care we need that isn't being provided. You've just told me one of those services."

"Good. I'm glad to hear that," Mary said and sat down again. "We'll need them, even if there's not a lot we can do about them."

"What about those health scanners they used on us when they took us on the ships?" Amanda said and both Mary and Ann looked at her. "Don't you remember? They scanned us to check to see if we were healthy or not? I bet they have stuff up there we'd give an arm and a leg for down here."

Ann's eyes widened as she remembered that day.

"They did scan us with something, didn't they? I'll talk to Rager about it."

That might just be the perfect way to find out if she was pregnant or not for sure. "In fact, I'm going to head home and see if I can get in touch with him. I think we could use that scanner sooner rather than later, don't you?" Ann kissed each woman on the cheek and started to leave. She paused before she made it to the kitchen door. "If I get hold of one, I'll let you know. You can come over and we'll check you over, shall we?"

"Of course, Ann. Love you, baby, and thanks for helping."

Ann waved and almost ran to the door. She heard her guard behind her and waited for him to climb into the transporter before she started it. The drive home was quick, but she felt as if it took far too long. She tried to call Rager, but he didn't answer. It was early afternoon, he was probably in meetings, but she finally left him a message and asked him to call her back. She added the word urgent and hoped that would get his attention.

She sat there in their bedroom, with a book in her lap as she waited. Her boobs were still sore, and she felt a little nauseous, so she didn't bother with dinner. She didn't know she'd fallen asleep until later when Rager slid into bed beside her. She barely woke up, but she felt him there and knew he was home.

"What was wrong, my love?" he asked as he felt her stir.

"I need one of those health scanners. The dog is pregnant," she muttered to him but fell asleep before she heard his reply or even realized that she'd said something totally off the wall. Exhaustion pulled at her and she couldn't resist, not even a little bit. She didn't feel the way his hand cupped at her stomach, or the way he kissed her hair before he rested his head on his pillow. All she knew was the pull of sleep and knowing he was there.

$\mathcal{A}$ week later, she woke up to the sound of whimpering. She knew she shouldn't hear that sound, so she turned over and tried to find the source of the noise. She saw a small box on the floor on her side of the bed, with holes all around it. Something was alive in it, and from the sounds it was making, it wanted out.

Her heart did all sorts of flips as she pulled the tabs open on the box to reveal a tiny chihuahua puppy. Its little head poked up, curious to find out what had just happened, and then it scrabbled its way out of the box. Ann was in love at first sight. She picked up the little black and tan puppy and laughed when the little bundle of energy squirmed all over her to inspect its new place in life.

"I think you need water and to go outside," she said to the still squirmy creature and put on a robe as best she could so she could go out to the balcony. She set the puppy down and found a small dish of water and food were already out there. The puppy inspected them but decided that exploring was far more pressing than food or water at the moment. "What am I going to do with you?"

The puppy yipped and jumped around and her little, semi-floppy ears perked. Ann had been able to hold off her squirming to note that it was a she, and she looked down at her now, more than a little befuddled. "What in the world made him decide I needed a puppy?"

The puppy yipped again and bounced around before she went back to exploring. She clambered up into the raised flower bed there, did her business, and came back and sat down in front of Ann. "That was convenient, but I don't think that was the proper place for that."

The puppy's head tilted but she didn't respond in any other way. "I'll have to figure out how to get you down to the ground to do your business, missy. For now, what shall we call you?"

Ann picked her up, set her on the table, and they stared each other down. Ann put her face down close to the little brown-eyed girl and jumped back when the puppy licked her nose. "I think that was a hello."

The puppy wobbled her head around but didn't do much else.

"You're no help with this, you know?"

The puppy stuck her head out and growled a little bit.

"Hmm." Ann watched her but the puppy didn't do anything but sit down and stare up at her. "I have to give you a name."

Ann picked her up and set the tiny thing, no bigger than her hand, down on her chest. She had all of her teeth, though they were tiny, and she had brown eyes, so she was a month or two old. Old enough to be on dry dog food. She was just tiny then.

"I could call you something like Tiny, but I don't like that. How about Katy? You look like a Katy to me."

The newly named Katy did more squirming and exploring before she finally settled in Ann's lap for a nap. "I don't know what I'm going to do with you, or why he gave you to me, but I'm glad he did. You're about as cute as you can be."

Ann needed to do some business of her own, so she scooped the puppy up and put her in her pocket. The puppy must have been very tired because she didn't protest or try to jump out, she just settled into the silk pocket and kept on sleeping.

Ann got through her morning routine and ordered some breakfast. She had a meeting with Skye later, and somehow, she was going to have to tell the other woman she hadn't managed to get a health scanner from her husband yet. She'd started to experience morning sickness, or something, the day after she'd been to her mother's and the exhaustion had started to spread into most of her day.

She now spent most of her day, and night, asleep, while the mornings were reserved for trips to the bathroom to empty her stomach. It wasn't so bad this morning, and she hoped that was the end of it. By now, she'd settled into the idea that her period wasn't coming and that she was more than likely pregnant. The way her breasts continued to swell and ache, along with the sickness, exhaustion, and lack of period were pretty good indicators to her that she was.

She wanted to be sure before she told Rager, and she kept meaning to send him a message about the scanner or to write him a note, but every time she started to, she fell asleep. If she could keep the puppy quiet this morning, she'd send him a thank you message and ask him for equipment for the clinic.

Ann walked around with the puppy in her pocket, and it made her smile every time she realized the weight against her hip in the square pocket on the front of her robe was the little dog. Katy, a good name for a dog. Now, she needed to figure out a name for her baby.

Her hand went over the flat of her stomach, no sign of a baby in sight yet, but she just knew. Something told her, some instinct far more than the symptoms of pregnancy she'd experienced, that there was now more in the world to protect than herself. She nibbled at some strawberries, had a sweet but plain muffin, and drank some grape juice. The grape juice was the newest addition to their pantry. She loved every drop of it.

Her smartwatch dinged, and she looked down at it. A reminder than Skye would soon be here. She went to the closet and found a long sapphire blue blouse that had similar pockets to her robe and a pair of shorts, and changed into those. The puppy stayed awake a little longer this time and stuck her head out of the pocket. When she saw Ann she yipped, and then curled back into the same position she'd been in earlier.

"Yeah, well, you might want to stay hidden down there. I expect Miss Skye is bringing the fire down on me today, for not getting the equipment we need yet." Not that anybody had made any progress. Meg still hadn't sorted the problem at the lab, but she had been able to give Ann's mother an ultrasound.

Ann had been relieved to learn that her mother was fine, but shocked to find out she was pregnant with twins. A boy and a girl. Better her mother than her, Ann decided with a laugh. She wasn't sure she could handle one baby, much less two right now. She had no clue what to do with babies, but she'd get some practice in with the twins, she hoped.

Now, if she could just stay awake today… she had to put that thought on hold as the need to get rid of her breakfast overwhelmed her. She ran for the bathroom and had just flushed the toilet when Skye showed up. "The butler let me in. Or whatever he is."

"That's fine. I'm sorry. Just a bit ill this morning." Ann reached over for a washcloth from a stack on the countertop and wet it down. She wiped her face and glanced up at Skye. "Remind me not to have grape juice until this has finished."

She stood up, brushed her teeth, and took a deep breath. "I'm not sure that's over, but I hope so."

"I don't think we need that health scanner, do we?" Skye looked at Ann with a new level of pity and concern. "Maybe some toast?"

"Did your books tell you that?" Ann went out to the balcony, her gait a little unsteady, but she made it. "I'll try anything at this point if it makes it stop."

"It might help. And something like weak tea. Just to make sure your throat isn't too dry."

"Okay, I'll send down for it. Want anything?"

"Chocolate cake, pineapple upside down cake, cheese danishes?" Skye smiled but looked at Ann with new concern when Ann's pocket yelped. "What is that?"

"That," Ann said as she reached down and pulled Katy out of her pocket, "is apparently the health scanner I asked for. Rager sent me a message while I was being sick. Said I asked for a health scanner because the dog was pregnant when he came home one night. He took that to mean I wanted a puppy. I named her Katy."

"Oh, my word, she is precious!" Skye cooed over the puppy, who pulled her head back and inspected the woman. Skye held Katy on her chest and close to her face. "I think you're just adorable."

Katy jerked her head in the direction of Ann and yipped. "I think you're also attached to your mommy already."

Skye handed Katy back to Ann and the puppy wiggled with frantic joy. "It looks like you're right, Skye."

"You have a stalker for life now," Skye laughed. "Puppies are almost like having babies. Only they never grow up. Not really. They stalk you forever."

"I've never had a pet. Mom and Dad were always too busy with work, and I was too busy with school. I'm not sure what to do with her."

"You'll have to get them to build you a staircase so you can let her outside when she wants to go." Skye pointed at the other end of the balcony. "That'll make life easier on both of you."

"That's not a bad idea. I'll suggest it to the men later. For today, she's been using the flower bed. I imagine the gardener is going to love her."

They both laughed at that, and Ann looked around. "My mom is pregnant, did I tell you?"

"No, but Meg did." Skye looked at her with a little guilt on her face. "It wasn't breaking patient confidentiality, not when we'll both be caring for her."

"It's okay, I'm just excited about it for her. Twins. My dad will go insane!"

"From what I've read, it can happen later in life, and your mom is in her 40s. So, it isn't out of the realm of possibilities."

"I suppose not. I'm just glad it's her. I'd die."

"No, you wouldn't. You'd cope, the same as she will. Women are always so afraid with new babies, but you soon settle into it. Don't get me wrong, some don't and weren't very good at it, but that was an exception to the rule. It wasn't the norm."

"You've learned a lot the last few weeks."

"Some of it I knew before, and I did do a lot of reading in that basement. I'm full of useless knowledge, but it comes in handy every now and then." She closed her eyes and put her hand over her forehead. "I have a headache, sorry."

"It's alright. Do you want some aspirin?"

"I've had some, it's just this heat. And I heard there'd been fires, so maybe it's smoke too?"

"Could be, and yes, there have been, to the north of us, in the forests. There's been a fire department formed, and they're up there trying to put it out." Ann had heard that from her mother too, who seemed to have far more information than Ann lately.

One day, Rager was going to have to take a day off. One day, she'd have a definitive answer. One day, she'd get to spend some time with him. She just knew it. She missed him, even if she filled her day with duties, and people, and now a puppy. She missed talking to him and being with him. Most of all, she missed his touch. Damn, she craved his touch so very much it hurt sometimes.

Maybe tonight she could stay awake…

"Earth to Ann, come in, Ann?" Skye snapped her fingers and Ann shook her head.

"Sorry, think I drifted off there. I'm finding it very hard to stay awake anymore."

"I noticed. It should get better for a little while, and then as you progress, you'll want to sleep but won't be able to get comfortable… and…"

"Yes, stop there. I thought this whole thing was glorious, and you glowed prettily, and took sweet photographs holding your bump, and maybe peed yourself once or twice, and then 'boom', a sweet bundle of joy appeared in your arms."

"Not quite, even though I know you're joking." Skye winked at her and pulled up her bag. "I brought that book I mentioned. When you can stand to eat, you need to eat really well, okay? Get lots of nutrition in your body. And make sure you're getting food with folic acid."

"I will." Ann took the book and looked it over. It had a woman in a rocking chair on the front, a giant bump cradled in her hand. "All nine months are covered, huh?"

"Yep, and you'll want to read every page. You won't be so surprised by stuff that comes along, or happens, or whatever..." Skye waved her hand. "I have to go, I need to check on one of the other wives. She's not doing well with her pregnancy."

"Oh no, what's wrong?" Ann asked but then shook her head. "You can't tell me, it's okay. Thanks for the books and the company."

"No problem. Let me know when you get that scanner, alright? We'll figure out how to use it together."

"Sure. Have a good day, and don't work too hard." Ann waved her friend off and looked down at her pocket. "Now miss, I think we need to find a way for you to get outside when you need to go potty. Let's go talk to the gardener and see what he can do."

Ann spent the rest of the day arranging the business of stairs for Katy, and asleep. Katy woke her up more than once to play or cuddle, and Ann did her best, but she was struggling to stay awake. It wasn't easy, but she did manage to see Rager for about five minutes before she passed out later that night.

She was certain she asked for a scanner properly this

time and went to sleep happy. He came to bed, kissed her with a passion she'd missed dearly, and then she fell back against her pillows, too exhausted to stay awake. She felt two presences as she slept now, one was her husband curled up behind her, and the other was Katy, curled into her stomach. Warm, safe, and loved.

$\mathcal{A}$nn got up the next day and took Katy outside for a walk and to chase leaves for a little while. She was so little she disappeared when she dove into a flowerbed, chasing something. More than likely a bee, Ann thought. The aliens had revived many of the insects needed for pollination and other useful things. Others had simply come back on their own somehow.

She let Katy play while she had breakfast and checked over her plans for the day. Skye had taken a test Meg created and had passed it with flying colors. Meg had been impressed enough that she had allowed Skye to start classes early in the mornings. There were four students, so far, and Skye enjoyed it, but that meant Ann's mornings were now free. Katy filled up plenty of that time.

The nausea hadn't been too bad this morning, and

she'd had toast and scrambled eggs for breakfast, which might rebel later. Ann was still learning the process of morning sickness, so she stayed on the lighter side of most foods until dinner time. Although, lately, she'd spent most of her dinner times asleep.

She scooped Katy up when the puppy came up for cuddles and scratched her ears and back for her. They'd become instant buddies, her and the puppy, and Ann was happy she had her now. She was a very smart dog, little Katy, and had already learned to let Ann know that she needed to go out with three sharp barks and a shake of her head.

Ann tried to think of something to fill her morning with today but couldn't think of much. Skye would come by after lunch, but there wasn't much else on her agenda other than that. With a sigh, she went to get dressed and made sure she had on a blouse that had a pocket on it for Katy. She'd just have to go out and explore some more.

She headed in the direction of a shop where she'd spotted some baby clothes and other things a person with a baby might need. Katy kept her company as she drove the transporter over. Ann felt incredibly alone, even with Katy with her, when she walked into the derelict shop. The guard quickly followed in his own transporter and stood outside.

With her hand over the pocket of her pink shirt, she looked around. Baby clothes, bassinets, cribs, bottles, strollers, it was all there for the taking. She called in with her phone-watch and asked for a truck and a couple of men to be sent over. She let the guard know help was on the way, and started to gather things up into three piles, one for her mom, one for her, and one for the other new mothers to be. The third pile would be sent to a depot and they'd have to go pick out what they wanted from there.

Ann filled several boxes with the help of the two men that came, and those were loaded into her guard's transporter. She would put the boxes into their storage area at the house until she needed them. She filled 6 boxes for her mother, double everything as she would have twins, and the rest all went in boxes for others. By the time lunchtime rolled around, she was tired, ready for food, and Katy had explored every nook and cranny of the shop. She picked the puppy up, put her in her pocket, and thanked the men for their help.

"You're welcome. We'll drop these at the addresses you gave us and unload them for your mother. Have a nice day."

"You too," Ann said in an offhand way, and headed for her transporter. The trip home took only moments and she went up to her room. She crawled onto the bed and put her head down, just for a moment. She woke up to find it dark outside while Katy barked frantically at her shoulder.

"I'm up, little girl, I'm up. Come on, let's get out of here and find you a place to potty." Ann put Katy down and she followed as Ann went out the door.

A quick swipe at her face with a washcloth, a brush through her hair, and a shower would be nice, but Katy needed to go, now. She took her outside and ordered some food and a drink from the kitchen staff as she walked through. She had dinner, alone, again, outside with Katy.

Her mom was too busy most days to come over very often, and Skye was her only other real friend. She got along with Meg and some of the other women, but she liked Skye the best. She reminded her of the best friends she'd lost so long ago, and made Ann feel like someone really cared about her.

Not that Rager made her feel unloved, he was just... busy. Really busy for a man that was still newly mated. He had a brand-new empire to run, though, so she tried to keep the complaints down. He would send her messages, gifts, and the things she asked for every day, yet the one thing she really wanted, she couldn't have. A little more of his time.

She thought about Rex, and how she'd longed for him to even acknowledge she existed. Those days were long gone, but she remembered them well. It wasn't that long ago, after all. She'd wanted him to love her, as she loved him, but now she knew she hadn't even known the boy, she couldn't have really loved him. Not like she loved Rager.

She knew some of it might be pregnancy hormones, but over the last few days, she'd finally admitted to herself that she did love him. How could she not? She might be asleep when he came home, but she always felt it when he was in bed with her. She slept so much better, wrapped in his arms.

He was a smart man, a kind man, and he made her heart skip beats when he smiled or touched her. She wasn't exactly sure what love was anymore, but she knew what she felt for him must be love. She'd protect him with all of her might, and she'd fight alongside him against any enemy. She also knew that she'd give him anything that would make him smile, that would please him, and she hoped, she really hoped, this baby would really make him smile.

She imagined the way she'd tell him. It would have to be over dinner, so he wouldn't miss work. She'd have a dinner ready for him, and they'd talk until he finished his food. Then, she'd take his hand and tell him he was about to be a father. She imagined the smile that would beam across his face and that he'd take her in his arms. It made her smile, and her stomach flip-flopped in joy.

Her watch beeped and she looked down. A message

from Skye asking if she wanted company. Ann felt bad that she'd slept through their afternoon meeting and replied that she'd love some company. It didn't take long, and Skye soon walked through the backdoor.

"Hi there, sleepyhead," Skye called as she came over. Ann didn't get up, but she did kiss Skye's cheek when she came over to her. "I left you in bed this afternoon, figured you needed some sleep."

"I did. I spent the morning gathering baby things, and came home and crashed. Poor little Katy was about to chew my ear off to wake me up." The puppy yipped and then chased a leaf that blew across her nose on a breeze.

"That's good. Better than puking your guts up all day." Skye sat down in a chair and took the glass of tea Ann offered her. "I talked to two more women at the clinic today, both suspect they are pregnant, but it's still too early to tell if they are. Those baby clothes will come in handy."

"I'm glad. Although, it's probably going to keep you two busy when all of these babies decide it's time to be born."

"Hopefully we'll have the other women trained to help by then. We're focusing on obstetrics and gynecology for now, and the basics of caring for patients."

"It sounds intense." Ann leaned forward, aware now of how tired Skye looked. "Are you sleeping?"

"It's hot in my apartment right now, the power keeps going off and on over in my area. I'll live. And yes, the training is intense. It's mostly going to be a trial by fire for those poor women that I'm teaching. None of us will have hands-on training, not until the births start. We'll have to rely on each other a lot. And the books."

"You can do it, I know you can. You're a smart girl." Ann was positive about that. "Oh, do you want to stay here until the power is fixed over there? We have air conditioning. Our power is always stable, the men wouldn't dare let the power go out over here. I think we have some solar panels too, just in case."

"That's actually a good idea if you don't mind? I don't know how much more of that heat I can take."

"No, it has warmed up, hasn't it?" Ann fanned herself with her hand and got up. "Let's go inside before this heat knocks me out again."

"I'm right behind you. Come on, Katy, you little, ankle-biting terror."

Ann laughed at Skye's joke and the trio went into the living room. The fire was out today, unnecessary now that more homes and buildings were being used by more people. Ann kind of missed the fires, but knew it was better to not have to use them. She settled on a couch she'd had brought over from one of her explorations. It had one long section, and then another section that came out, like a bed. It was the most comfortable place to be downstairs, and she climbed on the gray and dark blue fabric to settle down.

"If I'm not mistaken, I asked Rager for a health scanner last night. I fell asleep, and I haven't heard from him today, so I'm not sure." She wiped hair away from her damp face and took a deep breath. "Although, at this point, I think it's obvious that I am pregnant."

She said that last part softly, so only Skye could hear. Skye nodded and looked at the door before she responded.

"That's good. We can use it at the clinic, and any other technology they can provide would be appreciated."

"I'll let him know. I should probably go up there with him one day and find out exactly what they have up there."

"I've heard it's like one giant city up in that thing. I only saw a little bit of it, but yeah, they should have some stuff up there we can use."

"You know, I look up at it sometimes, this giant dark blotch on the sky, and wonder how people could be so stupid as to think they can get rid of the aliens. I mean, that thing is massive, and probably full of weapons we've never dreamed of."

"I've heard that they aren't a military society, but they've had to fight off other planets, and have learned to take care of themselves out there. They can hold their own, so I don't get it either. There's no point in even trying to fight back."

"But that's it too, Skye." Ann wiggled around until she was comfortable and looked at the woman on the other end of the couch. "Fight back against what? Not having a Constitution anymore? Being able to live above the ground? Having food, shelter, and a life?"

Ann shook her head, completely lost in one of her favorite subjects. "I don't understand people. Or wolves. Or aliens, for that matter."

"I think you mean men," Skye laughed and let her head fall back against the back of the pillow, her long black hair in a silk pony-tail. "Most of the problems seem to come from men."

"As usual," Ann agreed and shook her head. Katy wiggled up her body and curled into the space between her head and her shoulder. Ann stroked her absently while the puppy went to sleep. "It makes me sad that they can't let us live in peace, it really does."

"Maybe they will, after a while." Skye looked around and leaned over towards Ann. "We've got some stuff set up at the hospital, down in the basements, just in case things get ugly."

Ann felt fear wiggle its way down her spine. "What makes you think that's necessary?"

"I'm hearing more and more about this wolf revolution. And there's mention of some of the aliens that want to take Rager out of power and make someone else the leader. They think he's insane to have mated with you."

"Oh, that garbage. I've been hearing that since we mated." Ann tried to brush it off, but Skye shook her head and reached out for Ann.

"No, I'm overhearing a lot more of it, and from some people I didn't expect. The kind of people that work for you."

Ann's brows knitted together. "Are you saying…?"

She let the words trail off, completely shocked. These people knew her, knew she wasn't unkind, that she wasn't cruel. Why would they want to see her harmed?

"I am. I'm not sure which one, but one of them is definitely passing information along. Information like how often you're alone here and when Rager is at work or out of the office."

"They're tracking us?" Ann's face scrunched up even more, anger mixed with fear now to make her body shake. "Fuckers!"

"Which might be another reason I should stay here. If you aren't alone, maybe they'll back off."

"But I'm always guarded…" she started but Skye interrupted.

"You are, but the guard isn't looking for trouble from the inside, is he?"

"I'm not sure I want to live like this. I'll be afraid to eat next, afraid it will be poisoned or something."

"I'd suggest bringing in new staff, maybe from the new people that were brought in." Skye looked uneasy, but she carried on. "I think it's one of the guys that does the gardening I heard the wolves talking about. I'm not sure which one, but they mentioned the guy had to mow the grass a lot."

"Are you sure it was at my house?" Unease made her voice shake. "Because I know who it is if it's at my mother's house."

"It's possible they got the info wrong." Skye brushed a stray hair back into place and looked over at her. "I go to this dive bar, a little hole in the wall, almost literally. I keep covered up, and out of the way, so I won't be noticed. If I sit in that dark corner they have there long enough, I hear things."

"I hope you aren't spending too many nights in that place." Ann glanced at her, but her thoughts were still on Rex. "I'll make sure Rager hears about it all. Maybe he needs to send someone down there instead of you taking chances."

"Sure. It would be nice if we had a decent bar to go to, though. After five years, some of those shitty wines are now pretty good. It would be nice to have a decent place to go to, just for a drink and to relax for a little while."

"Thanks for gathering information for me, but please don't go back there. It sounds dangerous."

"I won't. I found a bottle of vodka if I get desperate." Skye's straight white teeth were on display as she laughed and rolled away from Ann. "Now, let's just hope Rager can stop all of this insanity before it goes any further."

"I'll talk to him as soon as I can." Ann cuddled her face against Katy's soft fur and thought about her baby again. She wanted to give them both a good world to grow up in. She'd have to find a way to make sure that happened.

18

The next day, Ann had breakfast with Skye and then they went their separate ways for the day. Skye went off to teach her class and Ann went to her mother's house, Katy in her pocket. Mary swept Ann into her arms the moment she came in and Ann laughed.

"Happy about the baby stuff, are you?" Ann kissed her mom and hugged her back.

"I am, it's all wonderful. And I love the outfits. I almost forgot how fun it was to dress you up when you were tiny. It doesn't last long enough, that tiny cute phase."

"Now you'll get to dress two of them at a time. I don't envy you that. But, in a way, I do." Ann still hadn't told her mother her suspicions, but she would, after she told Rager. "Twins, it's going to be a lot of fun being a big sister to those two."

"I'm glad you're looking forward to it, Ann. I knew you would, but I wanted to be sure before I told you." Her mother let her go and a servant walked by. Ann noticed that Mary quickly took the note the servant handed to her and also noticed the insignia on it.

Those bastards had stationery?

Ann frowned and followed behind her mother to the kitchen, as usual. What were Amanda and Mary up to? They surely couldn't be working to overthrow Rager? He was her mate, and she had settled into life with him. She never complained, or said she hated him, she'd always made a point to express the fact that she was happy. So, if her mother and almost-mother were aware of her happiness with her mate, then why would they join forces with revolutionaries?

Ann sat down at the long table in the kitchen and watched the two women as they ladled up chicken and dumplings.

"Decided to forego vegetarian food today, did you?" Ann asked, just to break the sudden silence the note had created.

Mary looked a bit stressed when she set a bowl down in front of Ann. "Well, we found some cans of chicken that were still good, and some cans of flour were brought to us. The dumplings won't be the best you've ever tasted, but it'll fill you up."

"It will," Ann said, distracted by the way her mother turned away, a guilty look all over her face. Or was Ann just seeing guilt where there was none? Maybe it was coincidence that the insignia was the same as the graffiti she'd seen around the sector lately. Maybe the graffiti artist had seen the stationery and used that as a guide? Or maybe the graffiti wasn't a warning of menace but a social group?

But if that was the case, then why wouldn't her mother mention it to her? Ann frowned, her head too mixed up to really think about one thing for too long at the moment, and too full of worry about it all. She really needed to talk to Rager about so many things, but he was the one person she hadn't seen a lot of lately.

She ached she missed him so much, and she wouldn't have thought that was possible when they were first married. Now, she was fairly certain that one more day without him might kill her. But then, she'd thought that for a while now. Her thoughts scattered away, to memories of him and the kiss that she was certain he'd given her that morning. A sweet, gentle kiss on her left temple.

She only knew he'd done it because Katy growled at him menacingly, and he'd laughed before he petted the dog. He'd left her then, and she'd gone back to sleep, an intimate stranger that shared his bed and nothing more lately. She felt the heavy sigh as it left her lungs, but couldn't stop it.

"What's wrong, baby?" Mary asked and stopped the spoon on the way to her mouth.

The urge to tell her mother all of her troubles weighed down on her. She wanted to blurt out her suspected news, she wanted to tell her mom that Rager wasn't cruel, but he was distant lately, she wanted to explain how afraid she was about the many people that seemed to hate her. They all hated her for being mated to Rager, human, wolf, and alien, the ones that wanted to harm her. At least they were united in that.

She almost smiled over that thought. She'd managed to unite all three of the groups through hate. Of her. That wiped the ghost of a smile from her face. She'd have liked to have united them for any other reason, but this seemed to be the only factor that had united any of them at the moment.

Should she tell her mom about the baby, at least, she wondered? She saw her mom's hand against the swell of her stomach, and how she'd waited to tell Ann until she was sure. It would be cruel to get her hopes up, only to dash them if she wasn't pregnant, she decided. She'd wait until she knew for sure.

Hopefully, she'd hear something from Skye soon, and then she'd be able to tell everyone that mattered. She didn't want to admit it, but she was also kind of afraid to tell her mother at the house. She'd tell her at her own house, she decided, in her bedroom, where hopefully she couldn't be overheard. She didn't know who was listening at the doors, or at the communication devices that were on every wall here. It was best to wait until she knew for sure, she decided, and to do it at her home.

"Nothing really, Mom. Just a lot on my mind is all." Ann went back to eating but the dish wasn't as appetizing now.

"You have to eat, dear. Finish your food. I won't pressure you to talk to me, but if you need someone to listen, I'm your mother and I'll always be here for you."

Ann smiled a wobbly smile and picked up the spoon she'd put down. It wouldn't help anything to worry her mother, so she tried to focus on anything except how much she missed her mate. Her phone-watch chirped, and she looked at it. A message from Skye.

"Come to the clinic, right now. We have a health scanner!"

Ann's eyes went wide, she dropped her spoon, and stood up. "I have to go to the medical clinic. Uh, they just got some equipment in and I want to see how it works. Thanks for lunch, Mom. I'll see you soon."

"Ann! What's so important you have to run off like that?" Mary's voice trailed behind Ann, but she didn't stop. A definitive answer was just a few minutes away, she didn't have time to stop and explain. She'd call her later, she decided and adjusted Katy in her pocket before she brought the transporter up and flew away.

She tapped her feet as she pushed the control stick, her lips moved, but sound didn't come out. Excitement, concern about disappointment, and worry ate at her, but she pushed through it all. Part of her wanted to go home and hide under her covers. Pregnancy would change everything, and it terrified her, but at the same time, she'd started to get used to the idea. She all but knew she was, and she'd started to like it before that message from Skye. Now, all the worries and fear flooded through her.

She set the transporter down, took a deep breath, and got out. Katy wanted to get down, so she put the puppy down on the ground. She sniffed around in the grass very quickly, did her business, and then tiptoed back to Ann. Ann's foot was still steady tapping, but she stopped when Katy joined her. "We have to hurry, little girl, Mommy's got to find something out. Quickly. Before she chickens out and runs away home like a baby."

Katy didn't reply, she just tapped along beside Ann and looked around. Ann finally arrived at the clinic's main office and walked in. "Anybody here?"

"We're back here trying to figure this thing out," Skye called out to her.

Ann walked back into a smaller office and looked as Meg and Skye worked together. Skye read out the instructions and Meg hit the buttons as directed. Nothing happened, so Ann sat down in a chair and waited. Her foot started to tap again, and Katy whined to get into her lap. She picked the puppy up and put her down. Katy crawled up from her lap to the top her chest. She stuck her head into Ann's hair, down for the moment, and curled around her neck, her warm little belly right against Ann's skin.

Ann had become accustomed to the dog doing that quickly, and didn't think about it. She simply put her head down to cradle the puppy there and waited. "You two are about to kill me, you know that, don't you?"

"Sorry, just trying to get this combination right. Nothing I do seems to work." Meg handed it over to Skye, and the woman followed the instructions with the scanner pointed at Meg.

Lights came on, and a blue light came out of the scanner. There were a variety of sections on the scanner, as far as Ann could see. It looked like a much larger version of the scanners that used to be a part of the checkout lines in stores. The screen was around 10 inches long and four inches wide. It was almost too unruly for the women to hold and operate, but it worked.

"Perfectly healthy," Skye announced, and then looked at Ann. "You ready for this?"

"Can you hold Katy for me, Meg? I don't want her to get in the way." Ann handed her puppy over to the other woman and stood against the wall. She stood as still as she could, but just when Skye was about to start, she moved, her face twisted with worry. "Are you sure this is safe for the baby?"

"I don't know, honestly, Ann. I have to imagine it's fine. The baby is made up of the same cells as you, and it shouldn't hurt it." She looked at Ann and then spoke again. "Besides, I think they'd warn us if there could be a problem for pregnant ladies."

"Okay. Let's do it then." Ann took a deep breath and stood up straight once more. She held her head high and waited for Skye to start.

It took the other woman two attempts before the blue ray came out and scanned Ann from head to toe. Ann watched Skye's face for any signs of what the test revealed, but the woman's face didn't change at all. Skye watched the display screens, and nodded a couple of times, but she didn't reveal anything.

"Well?" Ann finally asked, her voice impatient.

"I'm still reading this stuff, hang on."

"What do you mean you're still reading? You declared Meg perfectly healthy in a second. What's on that thing?" Ann walked over to stare at the screens.

Words and charts appeared all over the surface. Several areas were lit up in red. "What's that?"

"Your blood pressure is up, but that might just be your emotions. You're also a little bit malnourished. I imagine it's from all the vomiting. You need some more B-vitamins, and some vitamin C would do you some good. It's this one that concerns me the most." Skye tapped at a small box that glowed red and orange. "Something's wrong, but I don't know what."

"Alright, we'll figure it out, but am I pregnant?" She needed to know, and she felt like Skye was messing with her. She knew the woman wasn't, but it still felt like it.

"I think you need to call Rager." Skye finally looked up at her. She had a smile on her face. "Because yes, you are most definitely pregnant. This shows elevated levels of the pregnancy hormones. And see here? That's the baby."

Another small screen showed a small smudge and Ann looked down at it closely. Almost like an ultrasound, the scan didn't show a lot, but there was definitely a shape there that she was familiar with from ultrasound pictures. Her baby. It was real. Her hands went to her stomach and her eyes filled up with tears. "My baby."

"Your baby, Ann. You really are pregnant my friend, no more need to stress about it now. You can scavenge all the baby clothes you want."

"We have to keep it secret until I can tell Rager. And I guess he'll need to tell his men, or something. I don't know. I'm kind of scared what will happen when they find out. You know those people aren't all happy about me."

"We'll keep you safe if Rager can't, Ann. Don't you worry about that," Meg said from behind Skye. "I'm sure he's more than capable of keeping you safe, but just in case, we have ways down here to keep you from harm. You and your baby."

Ann hugged the other woman, and then Skye. "My baby."

She looked down at the screen again, at the little blot that showed up there and smiled. She had a feeling she wouldn't stop smiling for days now. Not with that picture in her head. She took a happy breath and took Katy from Meg. She had to talk to Rager, today. No more putting it off, she had to talk to him. To tell him he was about to be a father.

19

When Rager sent her a message that said he'd be home for dinner that night, she knew her own messages had finally gotten across to him. She needed to talk to him, she'd written, she had news to tell him. Important news.

And not just about the baby, she thought as she set up the balcony for a romantic evening meal. There were all these rumors she'd heard and the things she'd seen. She wanted to talk to him about all of that plus how safe she would be once it was announced she was pregnant.

She slid a hand down her side, the slick feel of satiny soft silk sensual on her palm. It was a fiery red slip dress that she had found in a boutique. It had the name of some designer on the tag that she faintly remembered as being an expensive brand, but she didn't care about that. It was the pure sensuality of the dress that she was after.

It didn't hide anything from the viewer, and without a stitch of underwear on underneath it, she might as well have been naked, but she knew he'd like it. He would be the only one to see her in it anyway. She smirked at the thought of his face when he saw it, and moved the rosebud a little to the side of his plate.

Her hair tickled at the skin at the small of her back, it was the only curtain that hid the skin of her back from view. The dress was backless, another thing that had drawn her eye. The entire thing weighed less than nothing, but it went all the way down to her feet. It was a feather of material, but it covered her while it also revealed all the things she couldn't hide. Perfect really.

She checked on Katy and saw she was asleep, tucked almost underneath Ann's pillows on the bed, and then she sat down to wait for her mate. Her brain still wanted to say husband sometimes, but the aliens never used husband or wife. Rager had explained to her that those words relayed ownership, what they were was far more than master and slave, or property of any kind. They were mates.

To Ann, that seemed far more profound than the husband/wife terms. Now, if only she could get her brain to let the terms go. She smiled as she thought about it. Now, she would get some time with the man that was her mate.

For a moment she remembered that red glowing

light on the health monitor, but pushed it away. Meg had told her she'd find out what it was from the aliens if she couldn't find it in the pile of information they'd sent with the scanner. She'd let Ann know if it was anything important.

Her heart skipped a beat when she heard the door handle rattle. She stood up and went to the door that led into the bedroom from the balcony. Rager came through and the moment he saw her his tired face picked up in a grin.

"You look stunning, Ann." He held his arms out and she went to him.

The moment he wrapped his arms around her, she sighed in relief. The burden of worry on her mind lifted and she felt at peace again. He held her tight for a long moment, and then pulled back.

"Let me get a shower, and then you have me for the rest of the night. It's been too long since we've had any time together, and I've missed you." He kissed her sweetly and then went into the bathroom.

She was a patient woman, now that he was home, and she waited happily. She put some music on and read a book while she waited, but she didn't really see the words. Her brain was too busy to see words when it could conjure up how Rager would react to her news instead. She knew he would be happy, but would he be ecstatic? Would he twirl her around and shout or would he pick her up and hold her close?

So many romantic notions, fueled by too many romantic movies she'd watched with her best friends when they were teenagers. How did men react in real life? She didn't know that, she hadn't had the experiences most women had by her age, not when she'd been underground, so far away from other people. Like many of her generation, she'd been isolated, and life had come to a standstill of survival and little more.

Not that she'd had it as bad as Skye, she reminded herself. At least she hadn't been alone, or so totally unprepared. Her father had kept her safe, and she had other people to talk to. Just not many people of her own age. Just that asshole, Rex.

"Alright, darling, I'm yours for the rest of the night," Rager said as he came out of the bathroom.

Ann's mouth fell open a little as he came out. He had a long black towel wrapped around his waist and nothing else on. She could see very lucky drops of water that still clung to his tan, powerful shoulders. There were even a few drops down the broad muscles of his chest and on the flat plane of his stomach.

"Should I put something else on?" he asked as he dried his hair with a smaller towel. "You look so beautiful, I hate to spoil the moment."

"No, that towel is just…" she struggled to make her

brain work enough to find the right words. "You're fine. Don't get dressed."

She looked up from the flat dent of his navel and saw that his eyes were on fire again. She could feel how hot her cheeks were. She was embarrassed that he'd caught her staring, but she knew some of that heat was from what she'd seen. A man made for a lover's gaze. Her gaze.

"Shall we eat?" he asked, but his eyes were on her now, on the dress that he wouldn't even have to take off. He could just slide the material up her thighs, and taste her, she thought, feel her.

"Yes, we should eat," she said in a monotone voice because she wasn't really aware that she'd spoken. She could watch the fire that blazed in his eyes.

"Come along then, tell me what was so important. Or did you just want some time with me?" He came up to her and took her hand to guide her out to the balcony. She followed and blinked when she sat down, awareness of the world back in place.

"Both, I suppose. I haven't seen you in ages. And I have news." Her cheeks turned red again, and she took a sip of water, just to have a moment to conduct herself. "My mother is going to have twins."

She was nervous now that it was time to tell him. She hadn't planned any big reveal, or a fancy cake, nothing like that. She'd planned to just tell him and get it over with. He wasn't the kind that would really get into that kind of stuff, he was upfront about everything and just stated what needed to be said, so she would do the same. Eventually.

"Oh, that is good news." He nodded, pleased from the look on his face. "I hope everything is okay?"

"Yes, she's fine and so is the baby. She had an ultrasound, and that revealed the twins. Your health scanner made sure that they were all healthy."

"Ah, that's what you all wanted one for. To scan the women that suspect pregnancy?"

"Yes. We, um, we used it on me earlier today." She took another sip of her water, unable to meet his eyes this time. Her heartbeat picked up and her chest went tight.

She wasn't sure why she was so afraid, but for some reason, now that the moment was here, she was terrified of how he'd react. She knew the ultimate goal for the aliens was to reproduce, and they'd taken no precautions to prevent it from happening, but was it possible he would be unhappy about a baby?

"Did you now?" He went still, his eyes on hers. He didn't move, his eyes didn't go wide, in fact, they narrowed a little. "And what did you find out, Ann?"

"That I'm going to have your baby, Rager." She stated it bluntly, the way he did things. She examined everything about him again, waited for the glee, the joy she'd hoped for, but he just sat there.

A long moment passed, he didn't blink, he didn't say anything, he didn't move. She wasn't even sure he breathed for a long time. Then he did all of those things and leaned towards her, a smile in place.

"That's good news. Our child shall have an honorable place in the world, with a respectable line of descent. It will have a lot of duties to fulfill, and I hope the child brings us honor and hope, as I have tried to do in my life."

"Oh. Good." She frowned, completely disappointed, but unsure if she should show it. "I'm glad you're, well…"

"Shall we eat now? I'm rather hungry and I'd like to spend some time examining how that dress feels beneath my hands."

She nodded, let her head fall to hide her face, and tried to blink tears away. That was it? Some trite shit about honor and duty, and the baby's ancestors? The sole purpose of them being mated was to produce children, why wasn't he more excited? Was he not ready for children? He had been forced into the situation as much as she had, she could see now. Maybe he didn't want to have children.

Or maybe it was her he didn't really want to have children with. Maybe he agreed with those soldiers of his. Perhaps that was why he'd spent so many nights away from her. Maybe he was as disgusted by her as those men were?

"Ann? Are you alright?" Rager asked and took her hand. His face was concerned, so she picked her head up and smiled.

"I'm fine. I do have some questions about safety. I've heard about the men that want you to mate with a woman of your own kind. That they want to overthrow you since you haven't cast me aside."

"I'm dealing with that, don't worry. You and our baby will be safe. You just concentrate on taking care of yourself. And being delicious as you are right now."

"Okay. But I've heard about some of your soldiers joining forces with the wolves that want to revolt…"

He sighed deeply and took both of her hands. "Now, Ann, you can't listen to these rumors. They will drive you crazy. You have to know I am doing all I can to keep you safe. You are my mate, nothing can change that. Not some werewolves that want to rule the world, and not my men that can't keep their heads on straight. I will always protect you, even when I'm not here. There are people here that will keep you safe."

"Okay." She nodded her head and smiled at him. "I just want to be sure you know about all of this stuff. I keep seeing that stupid insignia on everything. It makes me worry."

"That wolf graffiti? That's some women's organization, trying to keep the men of your world in check. At least they have some sense. As do you, I've noticed. You've taken the bull by the horns as well and have organized quite a lot. You make me proud to call you mate, I don't care what anyone might have to say about it. Excuse me." A knock at the door interrupted him and he went to bring in the trolley that held all of the food she'd ordered for their dinner.

She still had them on a vegetarian diet and had started to think maybe she would keep it that way. He didn't complain and ate plenty of whatever she had prepared for them. Tonight it was a Greek version of a casserole she'd found in a recipe book, filled with all sorts of lovely things. They ate slowly, and Rager told her about the things he'd been doing.

There was another bunker full of people that they'd tried to rescue, but it was underwater in Louisiana. It was proving hard to get to the people because the water would flood the bunker if they opened it.

"Why don't you put something around the opening, drain the water out, and have them climb up?" She offered when he went quiet.

He looked up at her suggestion, ready to dismiss it she could see, but then he thought about it a little more. "That is not a bad idea, Ann. Not bad at all."

"Thank you," she smiled, pleased at the compliment. "I'm not just a pretty face."

She'd meant it in a comedic way, to make him laugh, but he nodded his head very seriously, in total agreement.

"You're not just a pretty face, you're a beautiful face, and quite intelligent too." He did something with his phone, typed a few things in, and then looked up at her. "And what's for dessert?"

There was chocolate cake, made with cocoa powder she'd scavenged. It had been hard as a rock, the powder, but the cook had grated it, and pounded it with a hammer until it was a powder again. It was nice, and the frosting made her eyes close it was so buttery and good. The hint of vanilla was from dried vanilla beans and some imitation vanilla sugar she'd found.

"That is amazing," Rager said, his face a mask of pleasure. "I haven't tasted anything like that before."

"It's a simple cake, something you'd make for a kid's birthday party or something, but yeah, it is really good."

"I think your world is full of delights I've yet to discover. But the main thing I want to discover all over again tonight is you, Ann."

"I hope you find it as you remember it." She gave him a sultry smile and put the last bite of cake into her mouth. She pulled the fork from between her lips slowly when she saw his gaze was on her pursed lips.

"I'm sure it's even better than I remember, Ann. You are incredible, after all."

She knew she wasn't a supermodel, or even as beautiful as he claimed she was, but he made her feel as if she was. She smiled at him again, and took his hand. The sun had started to go down, and Katy had learned to climb down the stairs the workers had put in at the end of the balcony. They had nowhere else to be, but right here with each other.

20

A low rumble woke Ann up hours later. It was a sound like thunder, but loud enough to wake her up. Rain must be on the way, she decided as she heard another rumble roll along. A good storm would be nice if she could stay awake for it.

She stretched, felt Katy cradled against her stomach, and Rager wrapped around her from behind. His arm was over her, curled around Katy, and all was well. She moved a little to ease the ache she felt in her hip, it had been a very vigorous night and she ached all over, but she wasn't about to complain.

He'd rocked her world with his very intense attentions. She'd been disappointed in his tame reaction to her news, but the way he'd worshipped her after dinner more than made up for it. Kind of. So, he wasn't as excited as she was, it would be alright. She took a deep breath, looked around in the darkness, but couldn't see any signs of lightning. Maybe it was still too far away to see, she thought, and closed her eyes.

Exhaustion pulled at her to fall back into the embrace of sleep. She wasn't just tired because of her pregnancy now, Rager had worn her out. She had every right to sleep the night away now. She fell asleep again, a smile on her face, to dream about a day when she was out playing with her daughter on the grass behind their house, Katy grown up and eager to play with her tiny human. A small child, about three years old, with her daddy's orange eyes, and her mommy's hair. That smile was all Ann's mom though, she'd just noticed when she woke up, screams and the sounds of explosion unmistakable this time. That was no storm on the way, somebody had decided to blow things up.

She reached for him in the darkness, her mate, her protector, but he wasn't there. She pushed up in the bed and tried to see him in the darkness. "Rager?"

Another rumble, closer, and fear coursed through her veins. "Rager?"

She said it a little higher this time, the fear she felt made it sound tight. She scrambled over the bed and found him busy on his side of the bed, his black cargo pants on but not zipped or buttoned as he looked for his boots. A loud noise, and then the night lit up as the explosion made her scream. Katy barked frantically at her side, and Rager jumped over her body. "Stay down, Ann. Just stay down. My men are on the way."

"What's happening?" she screamed to be heard, her fingers clutched at his naked biceps. They were too wide for her hands to wrap around, but she knew she could hang onto him if she had to. He didn't have a shirt on, she thought, as the sound of the explosion started to fade away. He needs a shirt, if something falls on him, he needs a shirt.

"You need to finish dressing, darling," she said, stupidly she knew, but it was some direction to go in.

The house shook with another explosion, and she screamed loudly. But she couldn't hear it over the sound of the explosion. She turned and clutched at the pillows beneath her head and pulled one over it to make sure it was padded from anything that might fall.

"Alright, get up. Hurry, put something on, anything. Just hurry, darling." He jumped off of her, threw his shirt on, and kicked his feet into the boot he'd found on her side of the bed. He stared out at the sky, lit with the glow of fire, and waited for her to move.

She scrambled from the bed, grabbed a shirt, a pair of pants, and threw on shoes. She didn't even take the time to put on underwear or a bra, she just threw on clothes and nothing more. She completely forgot about socks or shoes, as fear was now in control of her every movement. The urge to go, to hide wouldn't leave her alone, and finally consumed her. Smoke had started to filter in through the windows, and she coughed as he put on the rest of his gear. She scrubbed at her face and picked up Katy. The little dog tried to scrabble up to hide in her hair, but Ann kept moving and the dog couldn't perch there like she wanted to.

Ann put her under her shirt and cupped her to her stomach so she could hide as another explosion went off. Ann dropped down to the floor and Rager was there with her, to protect her, as he'd promised he would. He pulled her close to him, tucked her under his body, to keep her safe if anything fell on them. She trembled in his arms and sought out his scent with her nose. She pressed her lips to his neck for a moment, just to let him know she loved him, even if she had never said it to him.

"Come on, let's get down to the storage area. I have a safe room for you down there. Let's hurry, baby. Stay calm, don't run off in a panic, stay calm and we'll get through this. Now, follow me."

The news must have gotten out and they'd decided to attack tonight, she thought as she turned to him. Fear made her eyes wide, she could feel it, but he looked calm. Angry, but definitely calm, as if the world wasn't exploding around them. She inhaled a deep breath and nodded.

She took his hand and stood up. His hand swallowed hers, so large against the delicate bones of her hand. She was safe with him, she told herself. It didn't matter how much the rogue aliens hated her. He'd keep her safe. He'd promised.

Later, when this whole mess was sorted out and the rogues out there blowing up the world had been stopped, she'd tell him she loved him. She'd tell him about all the hopes she had for their future, and how she wanted a life filled only with love between them and the children they'd bring into the world. But right now, she had to survive, and that meant following her now silent mate.

He stalked softly in the darkness, careful to scan around every corner before he took them a little further through the house. One hand was in hers, the other held his light gun out, ready for any danger that came their way. They were near the stairs, and Rager took a moment to look down over the banister. He pulled back and cursed.

Noise downstairs meant they weren't alone anymore. The servants didn't stay in the house at night, Ann knew, and she was fairly certain it wasn't them anyway. Rager moved them back to the wall the banister was attached to and tried to look down. She knew he couldn't see anything, not from where they were. Soft voices, the shuffle of a foot moved too quickly over tile so that it squeaked, and the sound of furtive movements told them the house had been invaded. That wasn't the servants that moved down there.

Ann stood there, quiet, until a scent caught her attention. There must be a huge fire nearby, caused by the explosions no doubt, because the house filled with the acrid scent of smoke. "Rager, I think the house is on fire."

She whispered it softly, so softly she was certain he hadn't heard her. But his hand tightened around hers and she knew he had. He turned back to her, ready to say something but he stopped. Somebody, a woman, screamed downstairs before she cut it off quickly. The silence that came after was broken by the sound of gunshots. Something hit the floor, a body, the woman's Ann could only assume.

"Fuck, they *are* in the house. Hurry, Ann." Rager guided her to the staircase in the darkness, and all she could do was follow. He held out the gun-like thing that shot out blue lights that could kill. She hadn't seen it in action often, only once when they'd first been taken by the aliens, but she knew what it could do.

There were more gunshots downstairs near the back of the house, by the kitchen, quick and sharp, so it must have been automatic weapons. Ann heard men scream as Rager guided her down the hall. Suddenly, he pushed her behind him down to the floor and stood his ground as his weapon let loose with a volley of blue light.

"Die, traitor scum!" She heard a stranger shout from in front of them, but then he screamed as the weapon's volley hit him in the head. The body slumped to the ground, and Ann felt shock take hold. Everything went quiet around her, and she held Katy tight against her stomach. Rager tapped her shoulder and she stood up to follow behind him.

They walked a few more feet before she heard more bootsteps, and two determined-looking men came out of the darkness. More gunshots, more blue lights, more bodies, and they moved again. Ann was on automatic, her thoughts as staccato as the gunshots that came from the automatic weapons.

Rager had guided them down the stairs, through the hallway there, and down until they were almost to the living room. They were almost past it when something whizzed by her head. She heard the shot after it passed her head and the bullet embedded itself into the wall. She turned to stare at the hole, somehow darker in the dim light that came from the windows in the living room.

Rager turned instantly and shot at the man hidden in the living room. The assailant fell and Rager pushed Ann behind him, but she didn't move from his side. There was danger on every side, from every direction. She had no weapons to defend herself with, she could only rely on him, so that's what she did. She let him lead, and she walked behind him.

They made it past the living room, and down the hall to the storage area. He pushed aside her boxes of baby items, and the other things they'd stacked in the room, to reveal a panel that moved aside when he pushed another section of the wall.

"In there. You'll find food and water. Don't open the door, don't come out. There's a bucket if you need the toilet. I know it's not great, but it's all we have right now. Stay here, Ann. Keep our baby safe, alright? Keep you safe, for me." He kissed her deeply, quickly, and before she could even touch his face again, he was gone.

The panel closed, and she and Katy were in darkness. Katy's tiny frame shook against her stomach, like a butterfly trapped in a jar, and she pulled the puppy from under her shirt. She stepped carefully until she found another wall. She slid down to the floor, too afraid to do anything but hide in the cloak of darkness.

There were people out there, people that wanted to kill her and Rager. They wanted to take over this new world and didn't care what they had to do to get that power. Ann shook as badly as Katy did, but the puppy helped to soothe her.

Katy crawled up to her neck, and Ann stroked her gently. The caress helped to soothe Ann too, helped to calm her as she calmed the puppy. "We'll be okay, puppy. Daddy will keep us safe."

Katy whined, and another explosion shook the house all over again. This one was closer, and Ann heard screams this time. Screams that wouldn't stop, they just went on and on, until Ann covered her ears to block the sound out. "Rager, please come back. Please come back to me."

She said it softly, too softly to be heard, her plea to the mate she hadn't wanted. She wanted him now, she had for so long now. She loved him, and he was out there fighting off who knew how many people.

There came the sound of transporters, and then gunshots filled the air. People ran all over the house, around it, and all Ann could do was hide. She reached around her until she found a blanket on a shelf not far away. She took it out of the plastic wrapped around it and unfurled the blanket to drape over her body.

"Over here, get more men over here!" She heard Rager bellow outside, and then there was the sound of boots against the ground as they ran to the area beyond the wall that kept her hidden. She put her ear to the wall and listened. Gunshots, shouts, and the sound of warfare. Screams of pain, and another explosion. What were those bastards blowing up outside? There weren't many houses around theirs, it was one of the reasons Rager had chosen it.

"Somebody get Ann out of here, now!" Rager shouted, so close to her she could have reached out and touched him if the wall hadn't been in the way. She held her hand up to the wall and pressed her face to the spot, but she couldn't feel him. The wall and the battle kept them apart.

She heard a sound, the sound of an animal in pain, and thought about the animals she'd been given. Where were the horse and cow? Had their caretaker put them in their barn? Were they safe from all of this? Ann wanted to get up and check, but fear made it impossible to move. So, she stayed where she was, with her hands over her head.

A series of explosions rocked the house, and Ann heard more screams. The night, which had been filled with sensual release only a few hours ago, was now filled with the sounds of the dying and those in utter agony. What had happened to the beautiful night that was?

Katy shivered against Ann's neck, and Ann did the only thing she could do. She turned her face to the puppy and began to reassure her that everything would be alright. "You're with me, little one. I don't know what's happening out there, but you're with me, baby. I'll keep you safe. Don't you worry."

Ann kept up a steady stream of speech, and the minutes passed. Everything went quiet after a while and

Ann thought it must all be over. There was no more noise, and the screams faded away, as if the injured had been carried off into the night. Her own shivers had stopped, but she could feel that her heart still raced in her chest, as if she'd run a mile in under five minutes.

The sounds of boots on the floor, orders were shouted, and then there was the sound of rooms being torn apart. That's what it sounded like to Ann anyway. As if doors were being kicked in and furniture was being torn apart.

Then a noise and the panel moved aside. A light flashed down at her, blinded her, and she looked away. "Rager?"

"There you are, madam. No, we're not that alien scum. We've come to relieve you of that burden you now carry and restore the rightful place of humans in this world. To free you from his… *attentions*. Come with us, please. Now."

Ann's heart froze in her chest and she looked up. The light moved enough for her to see a thin, mean-looking face. And behind it, something that made everything else freeze in her body. Rex's face, covered in a nasty smirk, glared down at her with triumph.

Terror filled her heart, unlike any she'd ever known before.

Shift Quickie

2 Hard To Bear

Bearly Over

Bearly Wolf

Kill Order

The Alpha

Kane

Cade

Jacob

Destiny Of The Dragon Prince

Defying The Dragon Prince

Chamber Of The Dragon Prince

His To Take

His to Mate

His To Save

and more…

ABOUT THE AUTHOR

Selina Coffey is a romance writer who lives happily in London with her husband and son. She is a hopeless romantic who grew up always believing in love and she is not ashamed to admit this! It is this belief that makes her so passionate about writing crazy love stories.

A stereotypical girly girl, she loves shopping. So whenever she gets a chance and the spare cash, you will probably find her browsing online for the next pair of shoes to add to her collection.!

You can find her online at
www.selinacoffey.com

Contact her at
hello@selinacoffey.com